DEEPEN THE MYSTERY

DEEPEN THE MYSTERY

Science and the South Onstage

A collection of plays

Lauren M. Gunderson

iUniverse, Inc.
New York Lincoln Shanghai

Deepen The Mystery
Science and the South Onstage

Copyright © 2005 by Lauren Martin Gunderson

All rights reserved. No part of this book may be used or reproduced by any means, graphic, electronic, or mechanical, including photocopying, recording, taping or by any information storage retrieval system without the written permission of the publisher except in the case of brief quotations embodied in critical articles and reviews.

iUniverse books may be ordered through booksellers or by contacting:

iUniverse
2021 Pine Lake Road, Suite 100
Lincoln, NE 68512
www.iuniverse.com
1-800-Authors (1-800-288-4677)

ISBN-13: 978-0-595-37966-8 (pbk)
ISBN-13: 978-0-595-82335-2 (ebk)
ISBN-10: 0-595-37966-4 (pbk)
ISBN-10: 0-595-82335-1 (ebk)

Printed in the United States of America

Deepen The Mystery:
Science and The South Onstage

TABLE OF CONTENTS

Author's Note vii
LEAP 1
BACKGROUND 143
PARTS THEY CALL DEEP 217

Author's Note

"The purpose of the artist is to deepen the mystery," Francis Bacon

I love this quote. I think it speaks to a special magic and wonder I've always experienced in the story-telling process. There is a mystery at work in good art, and by agreeing to take part, as an audience member, actor, or designer, we are at work with that mystery. We are at work with the human experience, the wonder and passage of knowledge, the process of emotion and understanding. I try to translate that feeling of mystery, awe, connection, and humanity to the stage through my plays—whether that be in their theatricality, historical content, character arc, science, or southern culture.

The work of the three plays included in this first collection was a huge and transitional process for me as a writer. They represent the first plays of mine to be produced, as well as represent my early style. I am proud of these plays; proud of the work that went into them, the partnerships I had the pleasure of making to see them realized on the stage, and the voice I developed because of them.

I have thanked the individuals who were particularly important to the development of each play. However there are a few constants that deserve long-term credit for their support: mainly my family, friends, professors and mentors, and the Atlanta theatre community.

I hope you enjoy these plays as much as I have.

Lauren
Nov. 2005

INFORMATION ON PRODUCTION RIGHTS

If you are interested in producing any of the plays contact the author through her website: www.LaurenGunderson.com

LEAP

A play based on the "annus miribalis" of Sir Isaac Newton

By Lauren Gunderson
©2003

"All that we know is that we know nothing."
Proverb

CHARACTERS:

ISAAC NEWTON: The 25 year-old version of the famed thinker. He is brisk, brilliant, and private. Will fight if provoked, can be vicious and manipulative, alarmingly secretive.

BRIGHTMAN BAINS: 16 year old girl. Confident, brilliant, and creative but brazen, independent, and unbreakable. Will fight if provoked, dedicated to the cause.

MARIA BAINS: sister of Brightman. 12 years old, brilliant, creative, much more restrained and polite. The epitome of sweetness balanced by dedication. Should appear more fragile than Brightman but never less intelligent.

LUCAS: Isaac's manservant and friend. Younger that Isaac, patient, quiet, caring.

HANNAH: Isaac's mother, mid 40's, country wife, uneducated but strong

SETTING: Issac's study, one room filled with wooden furniture.

PRONUNCIATION:
Woolsthorpe = Wool-shirp

TRANSLATIONS:
French—Also! Your intelligence is so big that you can't even see your own ideas.
Greek—The man who doesn't heed the words of the gods is a shameful fool.
Latin—You think you are alone! It is not only me, or only you, but all of us that—

SYNOPSIS:
LEAP is a story of left and right brain power, friendship and relationship, desire and hope, being young and being brilliant, creativity and creation, art and science. Based on historical and scientific fact LEAP infuses myth, science, and biography into a new history of the greatest scientist of the Western culture.

Directed by Megan Monaghan, LEAP was first produced by Theatre Emory in 2004. It was developed at the Playwriting Center at Theatre Emory and WordBRIDGE in Florida. It was first published by the Playwriting Center at Theatre Emory.

Thank you to Jim Grimsley, Theatre Emory, Megan Monaghan, Michael Evenden, and Vincent Murphy.

-*The Play* -

- PROLOGUE -

(70 year old Lucas, 75 year old Isaac, Brightman and Maria overheard, silhouetted, or seen facing away; each in their own sphere, not hearing each other, except the Girls who interact.)

LUCAS:
I didn't understand things then. Couldn't. Too complicated…

ISAAC:
You can't expect a man, ONE man…to make it all, to…find it all.

BRIGHTMAN:
Love is stupid.

MARIA:
But inevitable.

BRIGHTMAN:
Inevitability is stupid.

MARIA:
But our duty.

LUCAS:
How to fit the world on paper. I just couldn't…see. But now…

ISAAC:
There just wasn't time to get to everything…there wasn't TIME…

LUCAS:
Those years in Woolsthorpe…It came to him, suddenly, thoroughly. And everything was different.

MARIA:
Let's go.

BRIGHTMAN:
Back. Go back. Once last time.

MARIA:
Don't start this again. Don't do this—

BRIGHTMAN:
I have to see him.

MARIA:
You have to move on—

BRIGHTMAN:
It's been long enough. He deserves something.

ISAAC:
Something…

LUCAS:
Some things only he could understand.

MARIA:
We've got others to take care of—

BRIGHTMAN:
But he's—

MARIA:
Done. Famous, knighted, and dying. It'll only—

BRIGHTMAN:
Give him what he's always wanted. Let me do that for him.

MARIA:
After what happened?

BRIGHTMAN:
After what I did. Yes. Penance.

ISAAC:
You can't…I can't see anymore….Everything is…

MARIA:
He really changed you.

ISAAC:
Gone.

BRIGHTMAN:
Almost destroying the world will do that do a girl.
You go first. Ask him if he'll see me. Tell him I want to apologize. Please do this.

ISAAC:
Please.

LUCAS:
But now, so many years since,…I think I see.

MARIA:
Alright. We'll see him. But quickly.

ISAAC:
Oh God. Please come back.

BRIGHTMAN:
Thank you.

ISAAC:
Please come…

(Pause)

MARIA:
(Speaking to Isaac now)
Isaac?

(Isaac hears. Lights to black.)

- SCENE ONE -
(Lights up. Night. 1665, Woolsthorpe, England. Brightman and Maria walk about the mostly bare room, placing letters—the poems—throughout the room during the scene.)

BRIGHTMAN:
(reciting from one of her letters)
I sense the passion, feel the pace.
The world wants to reduce.
The air, the light, and moving space
Into equations you…seduce.

(Pause)

MARIA:
"Seduce?"

BRIGHTMAN:
Yes…It's sexy.

MARIA:
"Seduce?" "Seduce" doesn't make any sense.

BRIGHTMAN:

Yes it does.

MARIA:

Not when you can rhyme "reduce" with "deduce" just as easily. Into equations you *deduce*.

BRIGHTMAN:

He's a man. It'll get his attention.

MARIA:

He a genius. He'll think we're stupid.

BRIGHTMAN:

Are you still talking?

MARIA:

We're not trying to marry him. We're trying to meet him.

BRIGHTMAN:

Let me handle this.

MARIA:

You handled Marlowe and look how that turned out.

BRIGHTMAN:

Things "turn out" when you're dealing with genius. There's only so much we can do.

MARIA:

Just don't let this one near any taverns.

BRIGHTMAN:

He's not exactly the tavern type. We'll be too busy anyway.

MARIA:
What time is it?

BRIGHTMAN:
1665. We've got to hurry, we only have fifteen months or so.

MARIA:
You're going to try and get all this done in fifteen months?

BRIGHTMAN:
Or so.
If we hadn't wasted all that time on that damn Italian we could coast. Now rush rush rush.

MARIA:
Get the *ball* rolling?

BRIGHTMAN:
The only thing we ask, ONE rule: DON'T RECANT.

MARIA:
We've got to be delicate with this one. This is the structure of the universe…the foundations of…

BRIGHTMAN:
No Pope, no problem.

MARIA:
Brightman…

BRIGHTMAN:
Are you saying we can't handle this?

MARIA:
Your world is just frictionless isn't it?

BRIGHTMAN:
Yes. Except for you, my precious bump in the road. Come on.
(Places the letter on his desk.)

MARIA:
(Snatching it off the desk)
NO. That's stupid.

BRIGHTMAN:
Maria, trust me.

MARIA:
That's even *more* stupid.

BRIGHTMAN:
If I can get Milton to pen that beast of a poem, don't you think I can handle the planets.

MARIA:
It's your flippancy.

BRIGHTMAN:
I know what I'm doing.

MARIA:
But you can't do it alone.

BRIGHTMAN:
BUT. When I'm right, I'm right.

MARIA:
You are? What about when you wanted to give the *Odyssey* to Cramius Plitus?

BRIGHTMAN:
Who?

MARIA:
EXACTLY.

BRIGHTMAN:
Oh come on. He was a nice guy.

MARIA:
But not the right one.

BRIGHTMAN:
But Isaac is. The timing is perfect, the mind is fresh, the world is ready. He just needs a push.

MARIA:
I'm just afraid you'll run him over.

BRIGHTMAN:
The only thing he lacks is time. Cambridge will recall him in exactly 15 months or so, he's still stuck on this *alchemy* business, and he's a social flop. So. Start smiling, give me the letter, and…

(Maria doesn't move.)

Maria.

MARIA:
(Clutching the letter)
No. I can't in good conscience let Mr. Newton see this letter if it still contains that flagrant grammatical and intellectual error. I wouldn't be able to go on any

longer as a natural philosopher and as a member of humanity. There is a balance in these things and this is not *stable*.

    (*Pause*)

BRIGHTMAN:

What?

MARIA:

"Seduce" is stupid. I'm not.

BRIGHTMAN:

Stop it.

MARIA:

Brightman. NO. "Deduce" or nothing. That's my decision. There's simply no way round it.

BRIGHTMAN:

Yes there is.

    (*She walks around Maria taking the letter as she goes.*)

MARIA:

Brightman!

    (*Maria and Brightman chase each other around the room. Noises of people approaching. Brightman hurriedly hides the final letter in the whole in the wall. The Girls hide. Isaac and Lucas enter carrying trunks and boxes.*)

    (*Isaac and Lucas unpack a small wooden chest in his upstairs room at home. Lucas, 20 years old, puts books on shelves, and sets Isaac's desk with papers and ink. Isaac, 25 years old, walks around his room.*)

LUCAS:

Shall I start the fire, sir?

ISAAC:

Yes, Lucas. And if you would, put the Greek ones on the shelf, the Latin ones here on the desk, except those, those go by the wall.

LUCAS:

Yes, sir. Good to be back, sir.

MARIA:

(Gently)
Isaac? Will you play?

ISAAC:

What?

LUCAS:

(Preparing the fire)
Good to be back, sir.

ISAAC:

Oh. Terrible to be back. This house is rife with…boyhood. Memory. Of all the times Cambridge had to go and give itself the plague, right in the middle of my education.

LUCAS:

We were lucky to be spared.

ISAAC:

No such thing as luck, only timing.

(Lucas moves away. Suddenly Isaac notices a sealed letter on his desk, opens it cautiously and reads.)

ISAAC:

The race for right is that of love,
Truth braves what must be done.
In you, for me, lies both above.

My mind and heart you've won.

> (*Isaac huffily discards the letter and returns to his unpacking.*)

LUCAS:

And these, sir? Your metals?

ISAAC:

(*Distracted*)
Hm? Oh. Over there.

LUCAS:

Yes, sir.

MARIA:

(*Voice*)
It's just a game...

ISAAC:

(*Holding the poem*)
Lucas. Did you see anyone...on the premises? Anyone...

LUCAS:

Not in the house, sir?

ISAAC:

Nevermind.

> (*Lucas moves away. Another letter appears on his desk. Isaac turns around, sees it, and reads it.*)

ISAAC:

The straightest line is adoration
Love's infused Euclidian glance...
> (*Hotly crumples the letter and discards it*)

BRIGHTMAN:
(Continuing, voice only)
Our eyes two points in concentration
In the heat of love-aimed chance.

(Isaac hears this, stops, whirls around. Lucas notices.)

LUCAS:
Something wrong, sir?

ISAAC:
Where did that come from? Who's there?

LUCAS:
You're tired, sir.

ISAAC:
Tired, yes. Long day.

LUCAS:
Shall I prepare your room?

ISAAC:
Yes.

(Lucas leaves. Isaac slips his hand in his vest-pocket and notices another letter inside. Isaac violently shreds the letter and tosses it in the fire. Satisfied he sits at his desk until…Brightman's voice…)

BRIGHTMAN:
(Voice)
With the grace of inspiration
Trust a God of truth.
Colours split and gravitation,
Cast in th' fires of youth.

ISAAC:
(Looking around suspiciously)
Lucas. Whatever game this is can stop.

LUCAS:
(Re-entering confused)
Game, sir? I thought you wanted to sleep?

ISAAC:
Just…from now on make sure to lock the doors. I don't want anyone inside. No interruptions, no people…

LUCAS:
Not even your mother? It is her house.

ISAAC:
Especially not my mother.
    (Looks around)
Are you sure there was no one about? When we came in?

MARIA:
    (Voice)
I bet you can't…

LUCAS:
No one, sir.

MARIA:
    (Voice)
I bet you can!

ISAAC:
I swear it seems…the walls are talking to me.

LUCAS:

Talking, Sir?

ISAAC:

The walls...

(Suddenly runs to a corner, touches the wall looking for a certain brick or plank. Gently brushes the dust, removes the brick. Retrieves a bundle of papers from the wall.)

Precisely.

LUCAS:

Sir—

ISAAC:

The only place that was really mine. A hole in the wall; A place for secrets. Drawings, sketches, designs for flying machines, balloons. I'd spend hours planning ways to escape this...life, this house.

(Showing Lucas one of the papers)

I was convinced if I built this one big enough I could really fly away. It was a giant lantern with a candle to heat the air, a balloon to catch the heat, and a bench to sit and watch this place fade beneath me. And I'd paint it red so everyone would know it was me. Isaac and his red balloon. Gone forever.

(Throws the paper away)

Childish fancy. Useless.

Well. Everyone needs a hiding place.

LUCAS:

Perhaps you *should* retire, sir. Long day, like you said.

ISAAC:

(Nodding)

Yes. Yes you're right. No good courting the witching hour.

(Isaac gestures for Lucas to leave. Lucas leaves slowly, concerned. Isaac goes to replace the brick in the hole in the wall, but sees another letter in the cove. Removes it slowly, almost terrified. Lays it on the desk, eyes it suspiciously like a snake. Finally opens the letter, starts to read—)

(When Brightman and Maria appear suddenly, Brightman with flair, Maria with polite reserve. Isaac doesn't notice. They try again, standing before him; he doesn't notice them. Finally Brightman slams the door. Isaac jumps, and can see the girls.)

ISAAC:

What in the world—?

BRIGHTMAN:

I sense the passion feel the pace
The world wants to reduce
The air the light and moving space
Into equations you—

MARIA:

(Covering Brightman's mouth)
DEDUCE!

BRIGHTMAN:

SEDUCE.

MARIA:

That's completely idiotic. *Deduce* is mathematical.

BRIGHTMAN:

Seduce is dramatic.

MARIA:

I can't believe this. It's always something.

BRIGHTMAN:

Would you let me handle this?

MARIA:
Oh. And let you ruin another one.

ISAAC:
Excuse me? What on earth is going on here? Who are you?

(Pause)

BRIGHTMAN:	**MARIA**
Isaac! It's so good to see you.	Isaac. I'm terribly sorry about this.
It's so good to meet you!	You must've had a long day.
Sorry it took us so long.	We'll come back tomorrow.
How's school?	

ISAAC:
(Completely disoriented)
Closed. Everyone's dead.

BRIGHTMAN:
What?

ISAAC:
Plague.

MARIA:
I'm sorry.

ISAAC:
Why—

BRIGHTMAN:
What?

ISAAC:
Are you here? At midnight. What are you doing? Who ARE you?

BRIGHTMAN:
(Preparing to be impressive)
Mr. Newton…
Old World thought has lost its prime
And new men will define the time
As we found you, so you will find
The forces that can leap the mind.
(Posing with flair)

MARIA:
I don't think it's working.

ISAAC:
You. Poets.
(Picking up the letter from the desk.)
Get out. Both of you.

BRIGHTMAN:
But—

ISAAC:
OUT of my house, gypsies. How did you get in here?

MARIA:
We should try again tomorrow…

BRIGHTMAN:
I don't think you understand. We are—

ISAAC:
TRESPASSING in my house.

BRIGHTMAN:
Yes but—

MARIA:
We'll come back when you're feeling better.

ISAAC:
VIOLATING my privacy.

BRIGHTMAN:
Isaac—

MARIA:
Everything's better after a nap…

ISAAC:
OUT.

BRIGHTMAN:
ISAAC!—

MARIA:
BRIGHTMAN.

ISAAC:
NOW.

BRIGHTMAN:
WAIT. We know about the mathematics.
   (*Silence*)
The orbits, everything. We know what you're thinking.

ISAAC:

How did you know about that?

BRIGHTMAN:

We know a lot more than that.

ISAAC:

Where did you come from?

BRIGHTMAN:

Galileo.

MARIA:

(*Covering up*)
Shhh..
The gift is not where we've been, but where we're going.

ISAAC:

I don't want students.

BRIGHTMAN:

We don't want teachers.

ISAAC:

What is it then that you want?

BRIGHTMAN:

To play.

ISAAC:

I don't have time for games.

MARIA:

You should.

ISAAC:

Don't make me make you leave.

BRIGHTMAN:

Don't make us let you do that.

ISAAC:

(Shooing them out the door)

I said I don't have time. I don't have patience, and I don't have any reason NOT to throw you straight into prison for trespass and…and thieving and…irritating people.

(Shuts the door on them)

BRIGHTMAN:

(Calmly from outside the door)

Let's think about that. If you were to throw us *straight* with enough force in any direction, toward prison or no, we would eventually reach the curvature of the earth and start falling down as things tend to do, but alas and alack, we would never reach the ground again owing to the direction of the fall. We'd keep falling and falling and eventually pass right over this very point of departure in our constant yet never complete descent. Now. Is that really the way to get rid of someone?

ISAAC:

What…did you say?

BRIGHTMAN:

Falling and flying feel the same. Don't you think?

ISAAC:

(Opening the door slightly)

Why are you here?

BRIGHTMAN:

You.

ISAAC:

What do you want?

BRIGHTMAN:

You.

ISAAC:

Who are your parents?

BRIGHTMAN:

Our parents? Um…

MARIA:

Jove.

BRIGHTMAN:

Yes! And dear mum is…

MARIA:

Eve…Evelyn.

BRIGHTMAN:

Yes. Jove and Evelyn Bains.

MARIA:

They're out of town.

BRIGHTMAN:

They're not important.

MARIA:
(Slipping inside the room)
You see. We are children, we are female. We have not been touched, spoilt, or guided by any institutions and we would like to offer this curiosity and collection of forward-thinking games to you to further your philosophic and scientific exploits.
(Holds out the Book of Games to Isaac)

ISAAC:
(Taking the Book)
This makes no sense.

BRIGHTMAN:
It doesn't have to.

ISAAC:
(A moment, then a committed reversal. Dropping the Book.)
Yes it does. YES it does. And you don't make sense. AND I…I'm dreaming. This is a dream. And I should wake up. I've got much to do. The orbits, the new—

(Brightman throws a book in the fire.)

ISAAC:
WHAT ARE YOU DOING?!

BRIGHTMAN:
Doesn't matter if it's a dream.

MARIA:
Brightman, you shouldn't…

ISAAC:
That's my—! How could you? I need that!

BRIGHTMAN:
Trust me. Complete hogwash. Besides. You don't need them anymore.

MARIA:
You need us.

ISAAC:
You have no idea what I NEED. I need my books. My work depends on—

BRIGHTMAN:
Us.

ISAAC:
My BOOK is in the FIRE! You destroyed…. My work…my
(Pulling the unscathed book from the fire)

BRIGHTMAN:
Looks fine to me.

ISAAC:
It was burning. I saw it.

BRIGHTMAN:
(Nonchalantly)
How odd.

ISAAC:
That makes no sense…

BRIGHTMAN:
It will.
(to Isaac, pointing at the book)
Look.

ISAAC:
(Reading the cover)
Philosophiae Naturalis Principia Mathem...What?

MARIA:
Brightman. Be careful.

ISAAC:
I must be going mad.

MARIA:
No comment.

ISAAC:
Very funny. This is not my book.

BRIGHTMAN:
Yes it is. Funny and yours. First edition, you could say.

ISAAC:
This is not the same volume. This is not the one that you threw in there.

BRIGHTMAN:
Yes and No.

ISAAC:
It can't be both. Where's my book? This is not mine.

BRIGHTMAN:
Isaac...

ISAAC:
WHERE is my book?! What did you do with it, you little THIEVES!

MARIA:
That's not very nice.

BRIGHTMAN:
We're not giving it back until you hear us out.

ISAAC:
Give it to me NOW!

BRIGHTMAN:
NO. And if you don't sit down and be quiet we'll set the whole place ablaze and you'll be just as useless as Ptolomey on opium. Pages burn—

ISAAC:
But ideas don't.

BRIGHTMAN:
Then you wouldn't mind if I—
(Threatens to drop another volume in the fire)

ISAAC:
NO! Don't—

BRIGHTMAN:
Then we agree.
(Brightman points sternly at his chair indicating him to sit. Isaac sits. Brightman sternly indicates his shirt, Isaac looks where she's pointing and she bops him on the nose three-Stooges-style. She falls apart in giggles.)

MARIA:
Focus, Brightman. We're here on business.
(to Isaac)
She gets very excited.

BRIGHTMAN:
Yes, yes, yes. Now. Mr. Newton. It's very simple. We need you, and you need us, and the world goes on.

(Silence)

ISAAC:
And…

MARIA:
And?

BRIGHTMAN:
And…well that's it…what do you say?

ISAAC:
What do I say? I say if you want to play, find a dog. If you want answers consult a library. If you want to save your wrists the bruise the stocks will give them when I have you arrested for arson and trespassing you'll return the book and leave NOW.

BRIGHTMAN:
We don't like animals, we're not afraid of you, and we don't need a library. We've read all the books.

ISAAC:
You've what? *You've* read them all?

MARIA:
Yes. Both of us. We split them.

BRIGHTMAN:
Maria took Aristotle, I took Ptolemy. Maria took Copernicus, I took Descartes. Maria took Euclid, I took…oh, what's his name…green eyes, cowlick…

MARIA:
Archimedes.

BRIGHTMAN:
THAT's it.

MARIA:
And that's just western philosophy. We're only 28. Collectively.

ISAAC:
(*Completely kidding*)
And what, by chance, do you think of it all?

BRIGHTMAN:
The cannon is a bit dry if you ask me.
Plato was hijacked by the Christians. Democritus was ignored. Descartes is a modern prophet but still caught behind the Pope. Galileo was right, Kepler is almost perfect and it's high time to move Academia beyond Aristotle.
(*to Maria*)
Don't you agree?

MARIA:
Mostly. We disagree on Descartes. I don't like him very much but he does offer much to supplant and has a lovely preoccupation with light.

BRIGHTMAN:
You are quiet Mr. Newton. Do we shock you?

ISAAC:
You disgust me.

BRIGHTMAN:	**MARIA:**
What?	What?

ISAAC:
Prancing around my study making carnival spectacles, sporting the façade of knowledge. It is not a toy. You are meddling in the delicate arts of much superior artists. How dare you taint their names with such immature ravings. How dare you threaten ME. You are—

BRIGHTMAN:
Quite blunt, Mr. Newton. We are offering you an invaluable partnership.

ISAAC:
For the last time: Get out.

BRIGHTMAN:
You know, this is usually MUCH easier. You're too damn stubborn to see what's right in front of you.

MARIA:
Brightman…

ISAAC:
I am brilliant and in want of my privacy.

BRIGHTMAN:
I am vital and not moving until you treat us like the formidable guests we are.

ISAAC:
I don't take guests, no matter HOW formidable.

BRIGHTMAN:
GOOD. Then we won't be interrupted.

ISAAC:
What do you WANT, child.

BRIGHTMAN:

A CHALLENGE.

ISAAC:

You are MAD.

BRIGHTMAN:

And YOU are missing the POINT.

ISAAC:

I'm not missing anything especially whatever FOLLY it is you're offering. I'm a GENIUS.

BRIGHTMAN:

So am I, YOU ASS.
    (*She throws something. It breaks. Silence.*)

MARIA:

Please. A bit of etiquette for the sake of science.

ISAAC:

A genius? A gypsy quack is more like it. You've got nothing but a lack that makes space for fantasy and foolishness. You are nothing but a brazen-mouthed, ignorant, coarse, common *FEMALE* child. You're a waste of time until you grow up and SPAWN something.

    (*Silence*)

MARIA:

Sock him.

BRIGHTMAN:

Mr. Newton. As a last beacon of civility and proof of my extreme competence I will allow you to choose your poison: French, German, Greek, Hebrew, English, or Latin.

ISAAC:

What?

BRIGHTMAN:

ENGLISH it is.
You are a pompous, exaggerated book worm reducing the world from global geometry to singular planes that make you FLAT. You are ill-bred, ill-mannered, and ill-proportioned. Your clumsy audacity, and violent hypotheses rank against that of that bastard who gave my man the hemlock, the Romans that burned my library—

MARIA:

Alexandria.

BRIGHTMAN:

—and the INQUISITION. You are a straight line in a world of OBVIOUS fluctuation…

MARIA:

French.

BRIGHTMAN:

Aussi! Tan intellegence est si grosse que tu ne peut pas voir tes idées.

MARIA:

Greek.

BRIGHTMAN:

Toisi ton theon logois ostris kluon apistos ouk orthos fronej!

MARIA:

Latin.

BRIGHTMAN:
You're better at this one Maria. Go on.

MARIA:
Singularis! Non mihi, non tibi, sed nobis—

ISAAC:
English.

MARIA:
...and together we can raise philosophy like a *red balloon*...high above the world.

(Crystal silence. The girls bow as if being reintroduced.)

BRIGHTMAN:
But. You must be dreaming.

(Pointedly, the girls start to leave. He stops them.)

ISAAC:
Wait. Come back. Tomorrow. At night.

(Beat)

BRIGHTMAN:
Certainly.

MARIA:
Certainly.

ISAAC:
And no more...poetry. "Seduce?" You're children.

MARIA:
(to Brightman)

I told you.
> (*to Isaac*)

I told her!

BRIGHTMAN:
Oh…Here. You may want to keep this for future reference.
> (*Gives him the book from the fire. The girls leave.*)

ISAAC:
> (*Reading the cover again*)

Mathematical Principles of Natural Philosophy…
> (*He opens the cover and a spring with a jester's head pops out bobbing like a jack-in-the-box. We hear the girls fall apart in giggles. Lucas enters*)

LUCAS:
Sir?

ISAAC:
WHAT? What?

LUCAS:
Sorry, sir. I thought I heard a commotion. Do you need anything?

ISAAC:
No. No I don't. I was just…thinking. Out loud.

LUCAS:
Anything I can help with, sir?

ISAAC:
(Rudely)
No. Goodnight.

LUCAS:
Yes, sir.

(Lucas leaves. Lights shift to the girls in their bed.)

MARIA:
Good work. Only slightly illegal.

BRIGHTMAN:
He was being difficult. I had to give him something.

MARIA:
Yes but…gravity?

BRIGHTMAN:
He's going to be hard.

MARIA:
So was Leonardo.

BRIGHTMAN:
But at least he was funny. This one would rather croak than laugh.

MARIA:
Maybe he needs more than usual.

BRIGHTMAN:
Meaning?

MARIA:
He may just need some people. Some friends

BRIGHTMAN:
Either way. The ball is rolling.

MARIA:
We must be delicate. This is the structure of the universe, the foundations of…

BRIGHTMAN:
What are you saying? We can't handle this?

MARIA:
Handle with care. Slow down. Be nice.

BRIGHTMAN:
Alright, alright, alright.

MARIA:
And no more book-burning. One spark and that place'll go up like London.

BRIGHTMAN:
I was just making a point.

MARIA:
Don't make one that's so…you know…

BRIGHTMAN:
Inflammable.

MARIA:
Flammable.

(The lights slip back Isaac who sits at his desk pensively. Suddenly he stands and rushes to the girls' bed. Brightman is awake.)

BRIGHTMAN:

Isaac...? What are you doing here?

ISAAC:

You said something tonight. Um...I just got to thinking...

BRIGHTMAN:

That's funny. I just got to sleeping.

ISAAC:

I'm sorry. This was stupid. I don't know why I'm here—

BRIGHTMAN:

I won't either until you tell me. I said something?

ISAAC:

Yes. This evening. You were yelling at me.

BRIGHTMAN:

Oh...yes. Was it in Latin or Greek? Because if it was in Latin you'll have to wake Maria, I have no idea what she said.

ISAAC:

No. It was you. I remember quite clearly.

BRIGHTMAN:

You do?

ISAAC:

Um...let's see...you'd just finished the "ill-mannered, ill-bred" part...it was right after you compared me to the Inquisition...in English.

BRIGHTMAN:

Oh. Yes. I said ah...."you are a straight line in a world of obvious flu..."

ISAAC:

Fluctuation. Yes.

BRIGHTMAN:

Does that help?

ISAAC:

Yes.

BRIGHTMAN:

Good.

ISAAC:

Flux…

BRIGHTMAN:

Oh, and I'm sorry I called you the Inquisition. I just get excited sometimes. You're much more handsome than any Roman I've ever—

(Isaac leaves very suddenly.)

You're welcome.

(Maria wakes up and turns over to look at Brightman. Brightman smiles at her.)

Here we are. And here we go.

(Lights down)

- SCENE TWO -

(It is MORNING and Lucas brings in milk and bread, moving Brightman's Book of Games to set the tray down. Isaac wakes and grabs at the book defensively. Lucas leaves.)

(Lights blink)

(It is MIDDAY and Isaac is pacing around the room a book of his own in hand. He flips pages frenetically. Lucas brings in tea and biscuits. Lucas starts to say something but doesn't as Isaac suddenly stops to write something down.)

(Lights blink.)

(It is NIGHT, Lucas is checking the candles as Isaac sips tea as he studies at his desk by the candlelight. Lucas exits.)

(Suddenly, Brightman enters the room wearing a mask and carrying a music stand, Maria is playing some instrument. She sets up the stand for Maria and begins humming and dancing along with Maria. Isaac stares in disbelief. She finishes, Maria claps adoringly. Isaac tries to quiet them.)

ISAAC:
(Looking at the door, harsh whisper)
Are you mad?

BRIGHTMAN:
Yes and no.

ISAAC:
It can't be both.

MARIA:
You'd be surprised.

BRIGHTMAN:
Now…as we are finally all gathered, how shall we begin our first night together?

ISAAC:
First?

BRIGHTMAN:
Of many. I thought this would be appropriately ceremonial, but let's drop the pageantry and get to the grit.

ISAAC:

Shhh...I'm actually...in the middle of something.

MARIA:

Oh no.

BRIGHTMAN:

You're quite at the start. Would you like another song?

ISAAC:

No.

MARIA:

Sonnet?

ISAAC:

No.

BRIGHTMAN:

Portrait?

ISAAC:

No...I don't want anything...Yes. Yes, I do. I want to be left alone.

BRIGHTMAN:

No you don't.

ISAAC:

Look, I'm trying to be polite but...I hate being bothered, I hate being disturbed, and frankly I'm starting to hate yo—

BRIGHTMAN:

Now, Isaac, really. You don't know us well enough to hate us.

MARIA:

Or trust us.

BRIGHTMAN:

Which is a very big liability in discovery. And we can't have that, can we?

ISAAC:

Discovery of what?

BRIGHTMAN:

You tell me.

MARIA:

But we can't do anything until we get to know each other.

ISAAC:

And how do you propose to do that? I've been told I'm a little distant.

BRIGHTMAN:

The Who Game.

MARIA:

Ohh…Good idea. We've got all night and she's very good at avoiding silence.

ISAAC:

The what game?

BRIGHTMAN:

No, the *Who* Game.
   (Opening the Book of Games for reference)
This is a exploration of who you are by approaching you from infinite perspectives. Two players, but in this case we'll say three. The only rule is that the players can only ask questions that their partner has never been asked before.

MARIA:

Ready?

ISAAC:

No.

BRIGHTMAN:

Begin.

MARIA:

(*an interrogation*)
Do you dream in Latin?

ISAAC:

Uh…No.

MARIA:

Oh you should try it.

BRIGHTMAN:

Do you believe in curry?

ISAAC:

What?

BRIGHTMAN:

Do you believe that curry tastes the same to everyone?

ISAAC:

…Yes.

MARIA:

Do you like curry?

ISAAC:

I don't know.

MARIA:

I don't.

BRIGHTMAN:

Me neither.

ISAAC:

Look I really need to…

MARIA:

Do you celebrate your birth year or your birthday?

ISAAC:

I don't really celebrate…

MARIA:

But if you did, would you say, for example "Congratulations I'm another *day* older" or wait all year to say "Congratulations I'm another *year* older"

ISAAC:

The latter. Look…

MARIA:

Well…I suppose that's okay.

BRIGHTMAN:

    (to Maria)

Maria…

    (to Isaac)

Sometimes we have *opinions* in the Who Game. But we try to avoid them. It inhibits proper play.

ISAAC:
Girls…

BRIGHTMAN:
What's your favorite color?

ISAAC:
I don't have one.

BRIGHTMAN:
Yes you do.

ISAAC:
No. I….
    (Appeasing them)
Red.

MARIA:
Ohhh!

BRIGHTMAN:
Red…

MARIA:
(They think for a moment, then)
Crimson!

BRIGHTMAN:
Yes! Crimson is perfect.

MARIA:
(to Isaac)
Crimson?

(Silence, waiting for his approval)

ISAAC:
That's fine.

BRIGHTMAN:
Wonderful. Such a rich color. Mine is violet.

MARIA:
Mine is green. Do you play any instruments?

ISAAC:
No.

MARIA:
Would you like to?

ISAAC:
No.

MARIA:
Would you like *me* to?

ISAAC:
NO. NO. NO.

(They stop.)

ISAAC:
Are you done?

BRIGHTMAN:

Are you playing?

MARIA:

Is that your question?

ISAAC:

NO.

MARIA:

It's your turn.

ISSAC:

NO!

MARIA:

Oh….Game over.

ISAAC:

Yes. Game over. All of them. I'm sorry if I gave you the wrong idea— No. Actually, I'm not. Please leave. Go.

(The girls look at each other.)

BRIGHTMAN:

I don't think so.

ISAAC:

What?

MARIA:

No.

ISAAC:
But I…

BRIGHTMAN:
Don't really want us to leave.

ISAAC:
YES. I do.

MARIA:
Do what?

ISAAC:
WHAT?

MARIA:
What were you doing? That we came in the middle of? We don't have to play if that makes you nervous. We just want to know.

ISAAC:
(*Giving up*)
It's too hard to explain.

BRIGHTMAN:
Is it about the series?

ISAAC:
Yes. How did you..?

BRIGHTMAN:
Then it's not too hard.

MARIA:
Try us.

ISAAC:
(Pause, to himself)
I can't believe this.

MARIA:
But you do…

BRIGHTMAN:
…believe it.

ISAAC:
(Pause)
Yes. I suppose I…
(A wary silence. Snaps out of it.)
Polynomials in a series. That's it. Series…if I can just…I *can*. I just have to think…. You *see*, this is ludicrous. I can't explain it…

BRIGHTMAN:
Well you'll have to at some point.

MARIA:
Might as well…

BRIGHTMAN:
Would you like me to insult you again? Get the wheels turning?

ISAAC:
No.
(He laughs)

BRIGHTMAN:
(Smiling)
You laughed.

ISAAC:
Did I?

BRIGHTMAN:
Yes…go on.

MARIA:
Do you mind if we draw while you talk? It won't be distracting will it?

ISAAC:
No.

MARIA:
Good. Continue.

>*(The girls take paper and begin drawing on the floor. Isaac looks skeptical but begins pacing, thinking…)*

>*(Stage montage of Isaac thinking, the lights blink in between bits of his speech. Brightman and Maria continue drawing, increasing in intensity when Isaac does.)*

ISAAC:
If the expansion of *a* plus *b* to the nth power $((a+b)^n)$ yields what is already known through Pascal's triangle…then we must apply said theory to the quadrature of the circle beginning with the equation x-squared plus y-squared equals r-squared. $(x^2 + y^2 = r^2)$

(Lights blink)

ISAAC:
…expanded equaling y plus the square root of one minus x-squared OR one minus x-squared to the one-half. $(y = \sqrt{(1-x^2)}$ or $(1-x^2)^{1/2})$. But how to expand equations with fractional indices…the denominators will be easy, 1,3,5,7…but the numerators…

(Lights blink)

ISAAC:
(*With much more excitement*)
...in all of them the first term is x and that the second terms are as follows: zero over three times x to the third, one third times x to the third, two thirds...my god...intercalculated the coefficients of curves 1, 3, and 5 equal...the first lines of Pascal's triangle! My GOD.

(*Lights blink. Brightman and Maria are gone leaving their papers scattered on the floor.*)

- SCENE THREE -
(*Going to bed*)

MARIA:
(*Directly*)
Slow. Down.

BRIGHTMAN:
Please. I know how to handle people like this. Just let me.

MARIA:
Brightman, you've already given him the series. If I let you handle everything he'll have The Calculus by morning.

BRIGHTMAN:
It was a down payment. He was about to kick us out. *Again.* Then where would we be?

MARIA:
At Leibniz's door, giving him The Calculus.

BRIGHTMAN:
That's not the way it goes. We've got Isaac now. And now, thanks to me, he'll keep us.

MARIA:
Just keep a bit of pace, is all I'm saying.

BRIGHTMAN:
What is with the reprimand? We've only been here one night.

MARIA:
Just don't get *involved*, okay.... No more *seducing*.

BRIGHTMAN:
What are you talking about?

MARIA:
I know you.

BRIGHTMAN:
And I know this is right. He's *the* one.

MARIA:
(*Warily*)
The *next* one…. You mean.

BRIGHTMAN:
(*Caught, pause*)
Yes. Of course

MARIA:
Brightman…

BRIGHTMAN:
He is perfect though, isn't he?

MARIA:
(*Pause*)

He's pretty perfect. Which DOESN'T mean you can just—

BRIGHTMAN:
(A burst)
Oh thank god. Because I really do need your help on him. We've got to work together. The math is easy but the colors, and celestial mechanics, I—

MARIA:
Need to sleep.

BRIGHTMAN:
(Nods)
You know…you look very nice. The 17th century suits you.

MARIA:
Oh. Thank you. You clean up nicely yourself.

(The girls laugh. Lights shift to Lucas reading a book in Isaac's room.)

(Isaac enters. Lucas startles and stops reading.)

ISAAC:
What are you doing there?

LUCAS:
I was just reading, sir.

ISAAC:
(Pointing to the book)
That's mine.

LUCAS:
Yes but I thought—

ISAAC:
Servants are supposed to know what is and is NOT their business.

> *(Isaac grabs his book from Lucas. Silence. Lucas starts to leave. Turns...)*

LUCAS:
I was just...trying to understand.

ISAAC:
You needn't waste you time. It's far too complicated.

LUCAS:
I was speaking of *you*, sir.

> *(Pause)*

ISAAC:
Likewise.

> *(Lucas nods and starts to leave. Turns...)*

LUCAS:
Your mother wants to see you. She sent this note.
(Hands him a note)

ISAAC:
(Taking the note, looking at it quickly)
I don't want to see her.

LUCAS:
She came by yesterday. She's worried.

ISAAC:
Tell her I'm busy.

LUCAS:

You're always busy.

ISAAC:

Then tell her I refuse to see her until she can write a letter in coherent English. Tell her I don't care what she thinks I should do. Tell her I'm only her son on paper.

(Lucas doesn't move, pause)

Or lie. And keep the peace.
I've got to work.

LUCAS:

Sir.

ISAAC:

What.

LUCAS:

(Pointing to the book)
Are you...going to show that to anyone?
(Silence.)
It's just very...*new* and...I've heard what happened in Italy, and I don't want you to—

ISAAC:

Don't worry. No Pope, no problem.
(Catches himself, startled by his own statement.)
I mean...I'm not important enough to be dangerous.

LUCAS:

Yes, sir.

(Lucas starts to leave. Isaac stops him)

ISAAC:

I'm sorry. For yelling. You can…if you'd like to…borrow a book or two. For your…understanding. If you'd like.

LUCAS:

Thank you, sir.

(Takes a book and exits.)

(Lights down on Isaac.)

- SCENE FOUR -

(Brightman and Maria are decorating Isaacs's room in crimson adornments: bunting, pillows, drapes, tablecloths, etc. Isaac is at his desk working, doesn't notice. From the Book of Games,)

BRIGHTMAN:

The What If Game is a test in fantasy grounded in reality. A surmising process beginning in imagination and continued in applied theory. Start the game with "What if…" then continue toward the structure of the world today. Two players. Begin.

MARIA:

What if man created the world he inhabited? What if man shaped and defined the laws and look of the universe according to his aesthetic preference?

BRIGHTMAN:

Would we set the world on a schedule of evolution or perfect it in one consistent achievement?

MARIA:

Would the shapes in the world be geometric?

BRIGHTMAN:

Trees in straight lines, mountains as pyramids, rivers as perfect sine waves?

MARIA:
Would men themselves be symmetrical? All with perfect vision and hearing?

BRIGHTMAN:
Would all men be created equal or some destined to serve others?

MARIA:
Would we allow chaos? Free form? Chance?

BRIGHTMAN:
Would mountains crag, rivers twist, veins branch?

MARIA:
Would things erode, fade, or fall? Would perfection be the only option?

BRIGHTMAN:
And if we chose perfection, would we need art?

MARIA:
Or innocence?

ISAAC:
Or discovery....

(The girls spin around shocked that Isaac is participating)

ISAAC:
Would we have the knowledge inherently or would someone be chosen to find it.

(The girls look at each other, pause, then run at Isaac and hug him delightfully. Isaac grudgingly accepts the embrace.)

(Suddenly Lucas enters. The girls stop moving and talking.)

LUCAS:
(Going to the candles)
You shouldn't let them burn to the wick, sir. It's dangerous.

ISAAC:
(Viciously defensive)
Bursting in on people in the middle of the night is dangerous!

LUCAS:
I knew you'd be up, I was just concerned—

ISAAC:
And I was just in the middle of something very important, VERY important!

LUCAS:
You've been acting so strangely lately—

ISAAC:
All of which I've lost because of YOU. SO unless *you* can tell me the orbital patterns of Venus, you must get out NOW.

LUCAS:
(Terribly quiet)
I'm so sorry. I…Just watch the flames, Sir.

ISAAC:
Saint Peter. I'm not made of straw.
(Pointing to the door)
And lock the damned door.

(Lucas leaves extra candles then exits. Lights down as the girls relax.)

- SCENE FIVE -
(Isaac is standing paralyzed in thought…he is searching for an idea and nothing is coming. Brightman wanders around the room looking for…some-

thing. Finally, Brightman finds Maria under a table, and we realize they are playing a hide-and-seek game. At the same moment Isaac gets an idea and lunges to his book to record it.)

BRIGHTMAN:
Under the table *again*?

MARIA:
We don't have many options. Your turn.

(Maria closes her eyes, Brightman hides behind the lounge chair, Isaac is thrust back into the tip-of-the-tongue idea-search.)

MARIA:
(Noticing)
Trouble?

ISAAC:
It's what you get for making things up. No one to ask for advice.

MARIA:
(Glancing at his work)
Area?

ISAAC:
(Nodding)
Yes. Under a curve.

MARIA:
Under the…curve…

(Maria runs to the curved lounge discovering Brightman under it at which time Isaac recovers his idea and lunges at his book again.)

MARIA:
(to Isaac)
Right again!

BRIGHTMAN:
(Whining)
Isaac, stop doing that. You're ruining the game.

(Lucas knocks. Maria and Brightman freeze.)

BRIGHTMAN:
Not him again.

MARIA:
Don't start.

LUCAS:
(Entering)
Sir?

BRIGHTMAN:
(to Isaac)
Didn't you tell him to lock the door?

ISAAC:
(to Lucas)
Didn't I tell you to lock the door?

LUCAS:
Yes, sir. But that would require a key which would then make unlocking rather easy.

ISAAC:	**BRIGHTMAN:**
Ah Yes.	Ah, yes. Isaac, I'm thirsty. Do you want anything Maria?

MARIA:
Brightman, keep still. He's seen the book.

ISAAC:
Some tea, Lucas?

BRIGHTMAN:
He doesn't understand. Don't worry.

LUCAS:
Shouldn't you have something besides tea?

BRIGHTMAN:
Tea's fine for now. Unless he's baking?

ISAAC:
Tea please.
    (*Lucas waits.*)

ISAAC:	**BRIGHTMAN:**
What?	What?

LUCAS:
I'm worried about your health, sir.

ISAAC:	**BRIGHTMAN:**
That is not your job. Especially at night, you should be sleeping.	That's not your job.

LUCAS:
So should you. The body needs rest. So does the mind. Please.

ISAAC:
I think I know my own mind, thank you.
You'll do well to stay out of her way.

BRIGHTMAN:
You'll do well to stay out of my way.

MARIA:
No need to get pushy.

LUCAS:
Please take care of yourself.

ISAAC:
Saint Peter, you sound like my mother.

LUCAS:
She came again today. Your mother.

ISAAC:
What now? What does she want?

LUCAS:
Advice. Apparently your father is sick.

ISAAC:
He's not my father.

LUCAS:
She thought you might know what to do. She said she just wants to talk—

ISAAC:
Now she wants to talk. Wonderful.

LUCAS:
Shall I extend an invitation—

ISAAC:
No. Maybe she'll just forget. Invisibility isn't so bad.

(*Pause*)

LUCAS:
Do you think I could borrow another volume?

ISAAC:
Yes. You're welcome to anything you'd like.

LUCAS:
Thank you.

(*Lucas reaches for Brightman's Book of Games. Brightman dives for the book, Isaac snatches it quickly away from Lucas.*)

ISAAC:	**BRIGHTMAN:**	**MARIA:**
NO.	NO.	NO.
Not that one. It's in Latin.		
You wouldn't understand.		
Here.		

(*Isaac throws Lucas another book from his desk.*)

(*Lucas exchanges his borrowed book for a new one and moves out of the playing space. Isaac extinguishes his candles, closes his books, and pats the girls on the head as he exits. Brightman and Maria go to Isaac's desk, open his book, and conspicuously correct Isaac's writings.*)

- SCENE SIX -

(*At night. Isaac is writing. Maria plays with dolls.*)

BRIGHTMAN:
(*a whine*)
Isaac? Why must we always meet at night?

ISAAC:
That's our scheduled time.

BRIGHTMAN:
Yes, but why? Don't you *think* during the day?

MARIA:
(*Purposefully distracting*)
Brightman would you help me, over here?

BRIGHTMAN:
Gimme a second.

MARIA:
Now, please.

BRIGHTMAN:
(*Crosses*)
What?

MARIA:
(*Harsh whisper*)
Don't ask him that. It'll make him nervous.

BRIGHTMAN:
Why? I'm only asking about our "schedule."

MARIA:
He wants us here at night. The end.

BRIGHTMAN:
So you're his spokesman now?

MARIA:

He's working leave him alone.

BRIGHTMAN:

He was *my* idea in the first place. I can say anything I want.
(*Loudly*)
Isaac. Why don't we meet tomorrow at *noon*. We've been here long enough and we've yet to see the river. Tomorrow we'll play outside, under the apple tree. Then we can go to the bridge, or to the bakeshop. It's such a special day. Why don't we celebrate by going outside?

ISAAC:

At noon? No.

BRIGHTMAN:

Why not? It's our…

ISAAC:

At night, I don't see anyone.

BRIGHTMAN:

You don't see anyone during the day either. If you didn't have a manservant or a mother no one would know you were alive.

ISAAC:

Or care if I died?

MARIA:

(*Runs to him sympathetically*)
Of course that's not true.

BRIGHTMAN:

That's not what I meant.

MARIA:

She didn't mean it that way.

ISAAC:

I like nights. I can sit alone, I can watch the moon—and she is very important.

BRIGHTMAN:

What is it with you intellects and the moon?

ISAAC:

She is a constant reminder of the force outside ourselves. She is proof of order and priority. She keeps me thinking.

BRIGHTMAN:

Then what are WE doing here.

MARIA:

(*Warningly*)
Brightman.

ISAAC:

Things come at night. And they come to me. I feel…I'm doing something extra, something great.

BRIGHTMAN:

Something *secret*? Are you going to hide all your life?

ISAAC:

What if I did?

BRIGHTMAN:

It'd be stupid.

MARIA:

Brightman. He's not going to…

BRIGHTMAN:

If he hides himself he'll hide everything. That's not why we're here. That's not fair.

ISAAC:

Did I say I was going to hide forever? No. I said I was going to hide my *life*. No one needs to know anything about me to understand the planets.

BRIGHTMAN:

Why?

ISAAC:

Because, I don't need character to think.

BRIGHTMAN:

Well that's funny, isn't it—the public genius, the private man.

ISAAC:

I don't think it's funny.

BRIGHTMAN:

I think it's HILARIOUS.

ISAAC:

Why on earth is that hilarious?

BRIGHTMAN:

It's not a matter of what's on *earth*, Isaac. You should know that by now.

ISAAC:

You make no sense sometimes.

BRIGHTMAN:

That's exactly what I make.

(Maria glares at her.)

ISAAC:

Men have died chasing what I'm after. Sacrificed life and loyalty. It is NOT funny. This consciousness is as serious as you can possibly come close to knowing. You should treat it as such.

(Brightman looks down as though being reprimanded. Then bursts into giggles.)

You see! You've got no respect.

BRIGHTMAN:

Well, I think *you've* got know respect for making it so serious.

ISAAC:

It is already made how it is.

BRIGHTMAN:

You're telling me that when you realize the great coincidences, perfect tricks of nature you don't want to *laugh*?

ISAAC:

No.

BRIGHTMAN:

GOD DAMMIT, Isaac. THAT'S what's wrong with you. You can't follow the joke.

ISAAC:

God does not make jokes.

MARIA:

Oh yes he does. Have you ever seen an ostrich?

BRIGHTMAN:

There is irony in everything. Yes, there is order, there is pace, and measure but in those great things there is ordained humor. A sudden reversal, a *Yes* then a *No*. Without it…we are slaves.

ISAAC:

Slaves?

BRIGHTMAN:

To progress. And with it we are the reason for success. Isn't that right, Maria?

MARIA:

It's true. There's always a twist.

BRIGHTMAN:

Right. Now let's celebrate.

ISAAC:

Celebrate what?

BRIGHTMAN:

Our success. Our birthdays.

ISAAC:

Your birthday?

MARIA:

Yes the 25th. Your birthday too.

BRIGHTMAN:

WHAT a coincidence. Isn't that funny.

MARIA:

Congratulations to us all.

ISAAC:

(*Pause*)
Yes, to us all.

BRIGHTMAN:

How shall we celebrate, Isaac?

ISAAC:

Would you like some pudding? Or apple tarts?

MARIA:

I love apples.

ISAAC:

A basket then. And how about some Lady Fingers?

MARIA:

Yes! Please! A whole wagon full!

ISAAC:

Would you like that?

MARIA:

That'd be wonderful.

ISAAC:

Alright. We'll do that to celebrate our birthdays, our progress.

(*Lucas knocks. Brightman moves away from them.*)

BRIGHTMAN:
You see Isaac, we'll always be here for you. And always at night. When the moon is out. When you're at your best. When things twist.

> *(Lucas knocks and enters cautiously. Brightman eyes him, standing protectively near Isaac.)*

LUCAS:
Sir, if I could have a moment…?

ISAAC:
Lucas! Yes. I was just going to find you. I'm going to need a tray of Lady Fingers, a basket of apples, and three bread puddings. By tomorrow.

LUCAS:
Sir…

ISAAC:
It's a very special day, and…I'm suddenly very hungry.

LUCAS:
I'm leaving.

ISAAC:
What?

LUCAS:
Tomorrow. I've been of little use to you for the past three months. Just watching you, trying to…You can better use your money for…more ink, books, I don't know.

ISAAC:
You can't leave, Lucas.

LUCAS:
I can, sir. I've got an uncle in Shrewsbury, a carpenter who could find me work. The coffin business is booming these days.
Really. Besides getting in your way I just don't do much here.

ISAAC:
Oh, no. You do so much for me. You keep the outside out, so I can stay in. My mother, you keep her tempered. That's invaluable. You send me tea, and keep me fed—

LUCAS:
You refuse what I bring, make me lie to your kin, and treat me like a common pig—

ISAAC:
Then it is not your fault that you are unhappy. It is mine and I will improve. I must be a terrible master.

LUCAS:
Yes, you are.

ISAAC:
But if I gave you more to do, with more pay? Would that help?

LUCAS:
Sir, it's not the money—

ISAAC:
Because I need you. Now more than ever. Not just as a servant anymore. No.
   (*an idea*)
You must be the keeper of my writings. Yes. Correspondence, notebooks, journals. I'm entrusting my letters to you. I feel posterity needs to be taken into consideration all of a sudden. And you are the only one who…understands. Don't you?

(*Isaac puts his hand on the Book of Games. Lucas nods.*)

So you'll stay. As my secretary?

LUCAS:

If you promise to eat something, write a note to your mother, and spend at least half an hour in the sun each day…I will stay.

ISAAC:

Very well.

LUCAS:

Very well.

(They shakes hands. Lucas retrieves a small prismatic crystal on a string from his coat. Hands it to Isaac.)

I thought it'd brighten up the place. Happy birthday.
(Exits)

(The girls re-emerge. Brightman looks mildly betrayed. Lights down)

- SCENE SEVEN -

(It is night again and this time Isaac is waiting, staring at the door, waiting for the girls to come in. He has a tray of Lady Fingers, a basket of apples, and three dishes of bread pudding on the table. Out of nervousness, picks up the book of games, reads one aloud.)

ISAAC:

"The Yes Game. Only rule being that you must respond to each statement given with "yes" to continue the argument.

(Suddenly, Brightman rushes in delivering the monologue as she flits about the room. While ruminating the girls freely take from the sweets on the table Maria is particularly messy about it.)

BRIGHTMAN:

(In one didactic breath)
It seems that when fathoming the intricacies and patterns defining our universe we are only able to do so by making references to things we understand, primarily

ourselves. The seasons *change* as men do, the waters *run* as men do, the sun *rises*, the wind *blows*, and a joke most definitely *dies* as men most definitely do. We choose the same words to describe the world as we do to describe ourselves. Even in natural philosophy we extend our thought through mathematics—a man-made design for the structure of our man-inscribed world. Since it is *man*-made it is *man*-understood. It is supposed to be a method for our comprehension, our analysis, *and* we are men, THUS...we *are* what we want to *know*.

MARIA:

Yes. We are metaphors for the world.
    (*Kissing Isaac's cheek*)
Happy Birthday, Isaac.

BRIGHTMAN:

Yes. And the world is a metaphor for us.
    (*Doing the same*)
Happy Birthday.
    (*Continuing*)
That's why we create. That's why we design and innovate. That's why we control and dictate.

MARIA:

Yes. That's why we want to know things. We want to understand.

BRIGHTMAN:

Yes. And that is how we discover. We realize and accept the commonalities between the lives of men and the structure of the world.

MARIA:

Yes. But men's lives have not been structured the same over time.

BRIGHTMAN:

Yes...then we must first think of what is common among men. What repeats? What duplicates? What transcends time and culture?

MARIA:

Basic necessities?

BRIGHTMAN:

Yes. Food, water, shelter.
And…what results from having or lacking these?

MARIA:

Mmm…protection? Survival skills?

BRIGHTMAN:

Fear. Yes. Fear comes from that…and its opposite.
(Directly to Isaac.)
Love. And that's the answer. Love is everything, unconscious or designed. It is what is always and what is coming. Think of it. The emotion that drives, drains, and divides man…Love is our metaphor.

MARIA:
(Breaking the game and the dance)
Love? I don't know…I thought it was going so well until just then, with the love bit. I don't think you can go anywhere with it. What do you think, Isaac?
(Sits on his lap offering him a Lady Finger which he takes.)

(Isaac nods but isn't paying attention.).

BRIGHTMAN:

Not go anywhere? What about all the types of love? Isn't that right, Isaac. It's indefinable. Think of how many…shades of loving there are. Not even shades, completely different colors of love: maternal, fraternal, romantic, patriotic…An entire spectrum…all contained in one *white* word.

LUCAS:
(Lucas reads from Isaac's notebook.)
"White light being composed of every colour in the spectrum which can be separated through refraction devices…"

MARIA:

Brightman...

BRIGHTMAN:

(Slowly approaching Isaac until sitting next to him)
Or unrequited love. The kind that sends a girl sliding on the *curve* of emotion. Up and down with each glance and hope of mutual affection. The losing party trying to get so close but the closer one gets in the approach the more impossible it is to reach. Traveling further and further but never reaching, always *approaching the limit* of...

LUCAS:

(Reading)
"The limit of a function is the x value as it approaches but never *equals* zero..."

MARIA:

Brightman. Stop it.

BRIGHTMAN:

(Directly to Isaac.)
Take the basic, innocent first love. Two creatures so *attracted* to one another without strings or beams. The two lovers want nothing but to touch each other, to meet. Everyone's felt that attraction, that *universal pull* towards something, someone else.

LUCAS:

(Reading)
"The attraction of gravity being used to signify a force by which bodies tend towards one another, whatsoever be the cause."

MARIA:

BRIGHTMAN.

ISAAC:

(Isaac suddenly stands up, Maria slips of his lap)
I've...got something.

(Brightman stands.)

MARIA:
You're going too fast. This is too much!

BRIGHTMAN:
(to Isaac)
What is it?

ISAAC:
The moon…

BRIGHTMAN:
(Brimming)
Yes.

MARIA:
Brightman, I told you…

BRIGHTMAN:
Go to bed.

MARIA:
What?

BRIGHTMAN:
You need to go to bed.

MARIA:
You need to slow down…

BRIGHTMAN:
Maria, please. Do us all a favor: wash your face and retire.

MARIA:

(Wiping her face)
Someone has to be your nanny.
    (to Isaac)
Isaac…
    (Turns)
BRIGHTMAN.

ISAAC:

Please. I have to think.

MARIA:

I…you can't do this.

BRIGHTMAN:

Go.

ISAAC:

Maria be a good girl.

    (Maria protests silently. Grabs more Lady Fingers, then turns quickly and leaves)

BRIGHTMAN:

You've…

ISAAC:

…got it. The attraction…it's mutual…

BRIGHTMAN:

(Enamored)
Isaac. I knew it.

ISAAC:

The gravity of the earth is not her own gravity. It is…mutual. It extends to the moon…to mars…to everything. The attraction, the gravity…Everything depends on everything.

BRIGHTMAN:
 (Mildly disappointed)
Of course.

ISAAC:

But the measurement tables are at Cambridge…But I can take the estimate. What is it? 60 miles to one degree? Yes…60 miles would make the inverse…
 (In his nervous joy, begins to tear.)

BRIGHTMAN:

You're crying.

ISAAC:

It's so simple. It's perfect. Every time I open my eyes, it gets simpler. It works. Thank…God.

BRIGHTMAN:

What about me?
 (Catches herself)
I mean…Yes. He's very smart. God.

(Suddenly Isaac falls to his knees in prayer.)

ISAAC:

Lord of heaven and earth, creator, redeemer, ruler of all that is and will be. I am your humble servant.

BRIGHTMAN:
 (Echoing softly)
…your humble servant.

ISAAC:

Lord of truth and simplicity, I am meek in your favor. Lord of right and reason, I am blessed by your divine presence in every one of my motives.

BRIGHTMAN:

…every one of my motives

ISAAC:

Use me as thy tool, thy instrument, thy means. Keep me always by you, always of you, always for you.

BRIGHTMAN:

…of you…for you…

ISAAC:

God of great order, I fear thee as I worship thee. I know thee as I trust thee.

BRIGHTMAN:	**ISAAC:**
I love thee as I assist thee.	I love thee as I assist thee.

ISAAC:

I am your servant, your child, your mortal mind.

BRIGHTMAN:	**ISAAC:**
Take me in every way for thy glory.	Take me in every way for thy glory.
I am yours—	I am yours—

ISAAC:

…as your world is mine. Amen.

(They sit in silence, Isaac in triumph, Brightman in worship.)

BRIGHTMAN:

Isaac?

(*Isaac turns*)

Would you…hold my hand?

(*Pause*)

ISAAC:
Why?

BRIGHTMAN:
I…nevermind.

ISAAC:
Where is Maria?

BRIGHTMAN:
…Maria?…Sleeping. Well probably fuming, but in bed at least. You just said goodnight to her. Remember?

ISAAC:
Oh yes. I'm sorry, when I get thinking I…forget people sometimes.
  (*He laughs absently.*)

  (*Brightman smiles.*)

What?

BRIGHTMAN:
You laughed again.

ISAAC:
You noticed again.

BRIGHTMAN:
Can I ask you something?

ISAAC:

Is this another game?

BRIGHTMAN:

No. Just two people talking. Or we could dance?
(*Extending her arm.*)

ISAAC:

I don't dance.

BRIGHTMAN:

You should. It's just minding a pattern. You'd like it.

(*Slow music begins.*)

ISAAC:

I'm afraid I'm not a worthy partner.

BRIGHTMAN:

On the contrary…you're perfect.

(*They dance*)

BRIGHTMAN:

How do you think all this works?

ISAAC:

All what?

BRIGHTMAN:

This…passage. This knowledge. What we're doing?

ISAAC:
I believe in order, God. It is God's will.

BRIGHTMAN:
And...what is *your* will?

ISAAC:
To complete things. To know them completely.

BRIGHTMAN:
And if you...knew something was true, was right, *felt* right...even if it may defy the rules...you'd still try it, wouldn't you? You have to try...to see...if it was God's will or not?

ISAAC:
I suppose.

BRIGHTMAN:
You have to say yes before you can say no...right?

ISAAC:
I suppose so but—

BRIGHTMAN:
Then...say yes.
(She leans into to kiss him. He backs away.)

ISAAC:
What—What are you doing?

BRIGHTMAN:
(Covering up)
An experiment. A test. Testing...how things...fall. Maria wanted to know.

ISAAC:
Maria wanted what?

BRIGHTMAN:
Uhm. *Maria* wanted me to…test you. To see…what you thought about…falling things, things falling…in love. Because she heard that people *fall* into it…love. And she thought what with your current thinking on the gravity and other falling things that you may have some insight for her. On falling.

ISAAC:
Love?

BRIGHTMAN:
(*Of course, really talking about herself*)
Scientific love, of course. What do you think?

ISAAC:
I don't really—

BRIGHTMAN:
Because Maria, in her youthful resolve, wants to believe that…that she loves *you*.

ISAAC:
Me?

BRIGHTMAN:
Yes. Very much so. It's all she thinks about. It's a full time battle really. She desperately wants you to know, but she'd never *never* tell you. It's against her…spirit.

ISAAC:
Oh.

BRIGHTMAN:
And her spirit forbids it.

ISAAC:
Goodness. That is…awkward.

BRIGHTMAN:
(*Disappointed*)
What…do you mean?

ISAAC:
Love? It's bad enough as an adult much less a child. I feel so terrible.

BRIGHTMAN:
Terrible…of course. It's stupid. I tell myself everyday.

ISAAC:
Hm?

BRIGHTMAN:
Her. I tell *her* it's silly, childish. Very unprofessional.

ISAAC:
It's daunting, very…undefined. Distracting.

BRIGHTMAN:
I know.

ISAAC:
Very…tricky, deceptive. But then again what do *we* know about it. A scholar and a baby. Who would love either of us?
(*Laughs a bit. Brightman tries to.*)

BRIGHTMAN:
I take it you didn't like my metaphor then?

ISAAC:

What metaphor?

BRIGHTMAN:

Never mind.

ISAAC:

I wouldn't even know how to begin to explain it to the poor girl. Love is not something explainable, very unreliable…You must explain it to her. I don't want to hurt her.

BRIGHTMAN:

Of course.

ISAAC:

Love. What a mess.

BRIGHTMAN:

(*Suddenly*)
I'm tired. I'm going to bed.

ISAAC:

Oh. Well…I suppose it is late. Goodness how time fritters away.

BRIGHTMAN:

Yes. Goodnight.

ISAAC:

Thank you so much for the chat. I liked it very much.

BRIGHTMAN:

You're welcome.

(*Isaac uncharacteristically takes her hand in a gesture of thanks. She is overcome and runs away.*)

(Lights follow Brightman, who is quietly crying, to bed where Maria is waiting.)

MARIA:

You're stupid. Really, really stupid.

(Brightman leans over to Maria who hugs her tightly. Lights down.)

(Isaac nods off as lights dim to black.)

(Suddenly lights brighten as knocking is heard on Isaac's door. It is early morning and Isaac is groggy. The girls stumble on as well.)

ISAAC:

What is going on? LUCAS.

LUCAS:

Sir!

ISAAC:

Stop this at once—

(The door opens and Hannah enters, trailed by Lucas. Silence.)

HANNAH:

Isaac.

ISAAC:

Mother.

(Blackout. Intermission.)

- SCENE EIGHT -

(The same.)

ISAAC:

Mother.

BRIGHTMAN:

Mother?

HANNAH:

Isaac.

BRIGHTMAN:

Isaac?

ISAAC:

Lucas.

LUCAS:

Sir. She insisted. I tried to explain that you were busy.

HANNAH:

Son.

ISAAC:

You shouldn't be here. I'm very busy.

HANNAH:

Your family needs you.

ISAAC:

They're not my family.

HANNAH:

Your father's dying.

ISAAC:

He's not my father.

HANNAH:

Isaac.

ISAAC:

I'm very sorry that's he's not well—

HANNAH:

Dying, son. He's dying.

ISAAC:

And I'm sorry. If I can help, I'll try but…please leave.

HANNAH:

I've come because…You must run the estate. We'll move back to the house and you'll manage the farm. In time you'll inherit everything, have your own land, this house. As soon as your father passes…
Everyone's expecting you.

ISAAC:

No. I will not.
I'm going back to Cambridge. I can't stay here.

HANNAH:

It's your duty.

ISAAC:

Duty?

HANNAH:

As a son.

ISAAC:

Then make one of his sons do it. *My* father's dead. Or have you forgotten.

HANNAH:
Please, Isaac. You know there's only this way.

ISAAC:
I'm sorry. I'm leaving as soon the school reopens.

HANNAH:
Your father's already written to the school saying you won't be returning. He's explained everything to them. He—

ISAAC:
No. He can't do that.

HANNAH:
I'm sure they'll understand. A son's duty is more important than books.

ISAAC:
NO. I cannot stay here.

HANNAH:
Here or the debtors' prison. He's taken away your money, son. Cambridge doesn't care if you can't pay. And you can't as long as the farm's unkept.

ISAAC:
They'll let me in without money. They know who I am. I don't need you.

HANNAH:
Be realistic, son. This is the only place for you now. It'll be fine. You have a grand future.

ISAAC:
I've found my life! FINALLY. Let me have it!

HANNAH:

This is not a life, Isaac. It's a pen for dreamers. And even dreamers have to grow up. You've stayed in your head since you were a boy. Stayed in your head when the real world is hard and in front of you. You must face it now, Isaac. For me, for your family. For yourself.

ISAAC:

They'll have to let me back in if they know what I've got…if I can prove…I'll write to Professor Barrow. He'll understand. I'm a genius!

HANNAH:

You're a crazy

ISAAC:

I will NOT suffer this.

HANNAH:

What do you know of suffering?

ISAAC:

I know that my mother left for another life, with another man, in another house before I could talk. I know what a father's death, and a mother's abandonment does to a boy. I know what it's like to have only your mind for company.

HANNAH:

You know your *own* suffering, Isaac. You've never had any idea about the suffering of others. Your father—

ISAAC:

I DON'T. HAVE. A FATHER.

HANNAH:

You DID! He had your name, your hands. And I saw him die a few months before I saw you born. I appreciate your pain, son. I do. Trust me, I felt it. Appreciate mine.

ISAAC:

You can't do this to me. Not now. I'm no good on the farm anyway. I'll make money in Cambridge, send it back. If I become a Fellow I can support you. But I cannot do this.

HANNAH:

Everything I've done has been for you. So you could have land and property for your family, your future. Everything has been for you.

ISAAC:

Then keep everything. Because you cannot keep me. I'll find a way. I have to find away.

HANNAH:

Some men are born kings, some planters. It's no use tossing the order. You should move in within the month. If he lasts that long.
I'll send for you.
    (She goes to kiss his cheek. He flinches away.)
No more games, son. Become a man for us.
    (She exits.)

    (Isaac sits silently. Lucas goes to him. Isaac pushes him away. Lucas exits. Isaac turns to the girls.)

ISAAC:

Let's play.

    (Blackout.)

- SCENE NINE -

    (Isaac is at the desk scribbling. Lucas watched Isaac supportively. Brightman, trying to get his attention, is dancing as Maria plays an instrument. As Brightman's dancing and Maria's playing increase in speed and emotion, so does Isaac's furious scribbling. We should see a cohesive parallel in the pace

and motions of all three players. Finally, as Brightman and Maria finish with a flare. Isaac slams his book shut and stands with triumph. Isaac hands the letter to Lucas.)

ISAAC:

To Cambridge.

(Lucas leaves with the letter. Lights blink.)

*(Brightman and Maria paint on large pieces of paper hung on the walls. They use broad strokes of color that end up looking like a cross-section of a **rainbow**. Isaac is walking around the room setting up his **prism experiment**. Isaac lets in light which casts a rainbow on the wall next to their painting of the exact same image. At the same time:)*

LUCAS:

(From the book)
"Taking a Prism into a dark room into which the sun shone only at one little round hole in such manner that the rays, being refracted, cast colours on the opposite wall. The rays which make blue are refracted more than the rays which make red. Therefore colors are not qualifications of light but *original* and connate properties."

(Lights blink.)

(Brightman singing/humming. Isaac paces around the room, book in hand. Maria brings out a tray of tea and fruit, handing Isaac an apple. Brightman nods and Maria purposefully bumps into Isaac causing him to <u>drop the apple on the floor</u>. Isaac notices the fall but doesn't notice Brightman. She is noticeably upset and exhausted. At the same time:)

LUCAS:

(from the book)
"For it's well known, that bodies act one upon another by the attractions of gravity, magnetism, and electricity; but it is not improbable that there may be more attractive powers than these.

And to us it is enough that gravity does really exist, and act according to the laws which I have explained, and abundantly serves to account for all the motions of the celestial bodies, and of our sea."

(Lights blink.)

(Isaac is back at his desk with candle lit. Maria is on the floor drawing, Brightman is fast asleep on her lap. Isaac finishes, to Maria,)

ISAAC:

Well.

(Maria looks up)

I am completely drained.

MARIA:

That's wonderful, congratulations.

ISAAC:

We should sing something. Or dance?

(Maria points to Brightman. Isaac sees she's asleep.)

A chat then?

MARIA:

What would you like to talk about?

ISAAC:

I don't know. What do people talk about?

MARIA:

Uhm…weather? Music. Travel. Tell me about Cambridge? I've never been.

(Maria joins Isaac on the couch, Brightman rolls over in sleep.)

ISAAC:

Cambridge is...dedicated. To itself.

MARIA:

To learning?

ISAAC:

To whores and gin. At least the students are. I don't really fit in. It's become somewhat of a habit.

MARIA:

Whores and gin?

ISAAC:

Oh, no. Not fitting in. It's hard enough to think alone, much less around...over-excited boys. But the plague brought me back. And here I wait.... Here I wait.

MARIA:

(*a pause*)
It must be very heavy...your weight.

ISAAC:

How do you mean?

MARIA:

Well. You have great purpose and you realize it. That must be very arduous, all that pressure on yourself. You should delegate.

ISAAC:

Never. It is my job and God's gift. Solitary is the life of ingenuity.

MARIA:

You think you're alone?

ISAAC:

I've always been alone. To be a thinker is to be alone.

MARIA:

I disagree. Discovery is made of people. You are part of a line of progress. A line of genius that moves the world.

ISAAC:

A line is made of points and points are solitary and unincorporated. Don't I fit the part?

MARIA:

Only when you start to think you are alone, will you fade.

ISAAC:

Then that's my fear. Fading. Fading without anything…everything.

MARIA:

Everything is too much.

ISAAC:

But…it's so torrential sometimes…when every answer offers another question. Like a great ocean, a sea of unknowns, lies always ahead of me, and I'm a small boy on its shore, barely wet.

MARIA:

(smiling)
I don't know. That sounds fun to me. Playing by the ocean. Perhaps that's why you're good at it. It's different for you.

ISAAC:

What is?

MARIA:

Truth. It's fun.

ISAAC:

Perhaps.

MARIA:

Keep it like that.

ISAAC:

(*Pause*)
I like this very much. I don't know if we've ever chatted before, Maria.

MARIA:

No, we never really have. Brightman usually takes that honor.

ISAAC:

I suppose she does. In all honesty I was…a bit afraid of…your feelings for me. I didn't want to give you the wrong impression. Young minds are delicate.

MARIA:

My feelings for what?

ISAAC:

See. I've got no tact. Brightman mentioned once that you…

MARIA:

Oh dear, what did she say?

ISAAC:

Well I think it's very flattering but…it's nothing, it's youth.

MARIA:

Youth…

ISAAC:

I want you to know that I value you as one of my dearest most profound friends. But it can be nothing more, of course. The falling.

MARIA:

The what?

ISAAC:

Your interest in falling…in love.

MARIA:

MY interest. She told you that I…me and…!?
    (She falls apart in giggles)

ISAAC:

I didn't hurt you did I? I would do anything not to hurt you.

MARIA:

No. *You* didn't do anything. You just have to understand something about Brightman…she's always doing this.

ISAAC:

Doing?

MARIA:

Brightman has a habit of indulging herself. It might seem silly, just childish fancy at first but you must be careful. I've tried talking to her but she thinks you're different…Promise me you'll be careful. Don't let her, you know, get girly.

ISAAC:

I don't understand.

MARIA:

Me neither. Like you said, boys are just…over-excited. Nothing to get silly over.

Except for you. You're like a brother. An older brother. I've never had one of those. But we could pretend. Like a real family. You'll be the oldest, I'm the younger, and Brightman is…the pet.

ISAAC:
The pet?

MARIA:
A good collar and chain around that girl wouldn't hurt anyone.

ISAAC:
(*Pause*)
You seem different, Maria.

MARIA:
Well I'll be a year older tomorrow. Actually only a day older, but enough days altogether for a whole year.

ISAAC:
Your birthday?

MARIA:
Yes. Yours too I believe.

ISAAC:
My dear, you're right. I knew it'd gotten colder.

MARIA:
Yes. The 25th tomorrow.

ISAAC:
I'd almost forgotten. Age treats you so well, you barely look a day above…

MARIA:

Twelve?

ISAAC:

Yes.

MARIA:

Perpetually....It's part the game.

ISAAC:

As for everyone, I would think.

MARIA:

No. For you age is what you were, or what you will be. For me, it's…what I am.

ISAAC:

It seems hard. Does it make you sad?

MARIA:

No. It just makes me. To me a few years are a blink.

ISAAC:

Has it been that long since you came? A year or so?

MARIA:

15 months actually…Oh dear….

ISAAC:

What?

MARIA:

This is going to be difficult.

ISAAC:

What is?

MARIA:

It's time for us to leave.

ISAAC:

Leave? Why?

(A knock on the door.)

MARIA:

You've joined the line.

LUCAS:

(Outside)
Master Newton? Sir?

ISAAC:

What is it?

MARIA:

You have a letter.

LUCAS:

I'm sorry to've come so late, sir, but this letter arrived for you this morning. It fell behind the chest. I just found it now. I'm so sorry for the delay.

ISAAC:

A letter?

LUCAS:

Yes, sir. From Cambridge…a Professor Barrow?

ISAAC:
Barrow? My God.

LUCAS:
May I enter?

ISAAC:
Yes! One moment.
    (Waves at Maria)
Maria, Goodnight.

MARIA:
Goodbye.

BRIGHTMAN:
    (Groggily)
What's…going on?

MARIA:
Shhh…

BRIGHTMAN:
I must've fallen asleep…

MARIA:
Shhh…

    (Isaac opens the door)

LUCAS:
Thank you, sir.

ISAAC:
Please come in. Are you sure it arrived just today? It came today?

LUCAS:

Yes, sir. The courier brought it directly from Trinity.

BRIGHTMAN:

How long's it been?

MARIA:

15 months, since we came here.

BRIGHTMAN:

No. I meant…

MARIA:

I know what you meant. Don't worry…

BRIGHTMAN:

I'm not.

MARIA:

(Cold)
Clearly.

ISAAC:

(Holding the letter)
This is it. And if it's not a invitation, and if Barrow didn't understand, and if I can't go back to school…

LUCAS:

Sir. Read it first, then panic.

ISAAC:

Oh. Yes.

MARIA:

It's time.

BRIGHTMAN:

For the birthday party? Why didn't you get me up?

MARIA:

It's time…

BRIGHTMAN:

I know, did he bring us biscuits?

MARIA:

To leave. It's over.

BRIGHTMAN:

To leave?
    (Pause)
No.

MARIA:

Come on.

BRIGHTMAN:

No. I don't want to.

MARIA:

Too bad.

(Maria grabs Brightman. Brightman hits her hand away)

MARIA:

You can't lie your way into this. I know what you're thinking but…

BRIGHTMAN:

You don't know anything about it.

MARIA:

(A mild explosion)
BRIGHTMAN. I *know*. I *know* how this works. I *know* what's going on. I know what you did, what you told him.
You know you actually *do* need me. I *am* here for a reason. I'm part of this too, for god's sake.
There is a recipe for what we do. Challenge, passion, and balance. You are what is wonderfully savage about creation. That's why this worked. *His* genius and your hubris.

LUCAS:

I'm to send off a reply as soon as possible.

ISAAC:

Of course. Unless it's bad news.
(Reading)
"We have the pleasure of informing you that the College of the Holy and Undivided Trinity at the University of Cambridge will re-commence instruction on January 5th in the year of our Lord 1667."

MARIA:

But this is too much. You are too much.

BRIGHTMAN:

For *you* or for *him*?

ISAAC:

"You are hereby invited to take your place as a scholar of the house, which position will entitle you to commons from the College, an annual allowance thirteen shillings fourpence and a stipend of the same amount for the next four years!"

MARIA:

You're doing this to yourself.

BRIGHTMAN:

I'm a savage am I?

ISAAC:

"You may at any time, and I encourage this for you Mister Newton, seek election to a Fellow of the College."

BRIGHTMAN:

Well. How long have you hated me so?

LUCAS:

A fellow, sir!

MARIA:

You know I don't hate anything about you.

BRIGHTMAN:

This doesn't sound much like love.

MARIA:

Another thing that confuses you.

ISAAC:

A fellow. I could be…

BRIGHTMAN:

What is that supposed to mean?

MARIA:

Love is *not* compliment. It is honesty. It is friendship. It is energy towards understanding.

ISAAC:

It worked. I knew Barrow'd understand. If I just explained the situation, explained what I've been working on. I knew it.

LUCAS:

Congratulations, sir. You were right. A good idea carries.

BRIGHTMAN:

And have I been so lacking in those?

MARIA:

Yes. Your energy goes *to* him. Not *for* him, but *to* him like a flood raging. You're dangerous. You know he can't love you. You *know* it. You're writing the wrong history.

BRIGHTMAN:

Because it doesn't include you at every step? Is that why you're so adamant? I'm more of a woman than you? Jealousy fuels this fire, doesn't it, little sister?

MARIA:

I'm trying to protect you.

BRIGHTMAN:

From what?

MARIA:

Yourself. You are built to burn.

BRIGHTMAN:

Well. If you find it so necessary to hate me then I find it necessary to move on. I can't work in these conditions. He can't work in these conditions.

MARIA:

That's why he's leaving for Cambridge.

BRIGHTMAN:
What?

MARIA:
Listen.

ISAAC:
The school is re-opening. The world is re-opening.

LUCAS:
That's wonderful, sir. I should start packing.

ISAAC:
Yes. YES!

BRIGHTMAN:
What?

MARIA:
Our time is over. We're done.

BRIGHTMAN:
Why didn't you tell me this was happening! Why didn't you stop him!

ISAAC:
First write that I will most definitely be in attendance…AND that I've got much to show him. The binomials, Gregory and Slusius' and the…

LUCAS:
Sir?

ISAAC:
Yes?

LUCAS:

You should write that part.

MARIA:

You can't stop him. He's supposed to go to Cambridge. It's the plan.

BRIGHTMAN:

NO.

(Isaac writes his letter. Brightman runs to him and throws his paper on the ground. Isaac doesn't notice her. He simply retrieves another piece of paper and continues writing.)

BRIGHTMAN:

ISAAC! NO! STOP IT!

MARIA:

We have to let him go. They all have to go. I don't know why he should be any different.

BRIGHTMAN:

Because he doesn't love you.

MARIA:

And he CAN'T love YOU.

BRIGHTMAN:

Don't scoff at me, you TRAITOR. Why didn't you stop this!

MARIA:

We're fading, we're finished. Come on.

BRIGHTMAN:

NO NO NO!

> *(Brightman throws Isaac's paper away again. Isaac retrieves another. Lucas notices nothing.)*

BRIGHTMAN:

I'm not leaving. I'm NOT leaving him!

MARIA:

Why are you doing this?

BRIGHTMAN:

Why are YOU doing this, you defector?

MARIA:

You can't have him.

BRIGHTMAN:

Not while you're here I can't. GET OUT!!!
I. Don't. Need you.

MARIA:

Really.

BRIGHTMAN:

For the sake of progress, Isaac and I…

MARIA:

Are nothing. NOTHING. Without me you'll combust near him. I'm the balance. Don't do this, Brightman.

BRIGHTMAN:

I will. I will as much as you won't. He is the light for the world of thought and I am the fire. He is a gift to the world of knowing and I am the hands that offer him. He is…

MARIA:

Moving back to Cambridge!

ISAAC:

(*Finishing the letter*)
There you are. Send this off as soon as possible.

BRIGHTMAN:

ISAAC, NO.

LUCAS:

Very good, sir.

ISAAC:

Wonderful, marvelous, extraordinary.

LUCAS:

And your mother, sir? What shall I tell her?

ISAAC:

That any money I make, I'll send directly to the farm. And…tell her I'm sorry. And God bless.

(*Silence*)

BRIGHTMAN:

He's—

MARIA:

Made up his mind.

BRIGHTMAN:

WE make up his mind.
    (*Running to Isaac who doesn't see her,*)
Don't do this. You don't want to.

MARIA:

It's over.

BRIGHTMAN:

It doesn't have to be.

MARIA:

Yes it does. We've done what we came to do.

BRIGHTMAN:

What about what we WANT to do! Doesn't that count for anything.

MARIA:

NO it doesn't.

BRIGHTMAN:

I WANT to LOVE HIM!

MARIA:

You can't.

BRIGHTMAN:

Then I want to DIE.

MARIA:

You can't.

BRIGHTMAN:

Then I want him to die.

MARIA:

He will. They all will.

    (*Silence*)

LUCAS:

Anything else, sir?

BRIGHTMAN:

Oh God…

MARIA:

Very much so actually.
    (*Dryly*)
But you knew that. Or perhaps…you've forgotten that part.

    (*Maria starts to exit*)

BRIGHTMAN:

Maria. Don't. I'm sorry.

MARIA:

No you're not. You're scared.

BRIGHTMAN:

Maria, stop.

MARIA:

I can't. He's already forgotten me. Now say goodbye.

BRIGHTMAN:

Maria!

(Maria walks over to Isaac who does not notice her, and kisses his cheek.)

MARIA:
(to Isaac)
You've done very well. Goodbye.

(Maria vanishes. Brightman stares at the door after her. Isaac cannot see her.)

LUCAS:
Anything else, sir?

ISAAC:
No. But thank you, Lucas. For putting up with me. We've got a real start, haven't we?

BRIGHTMAN:
Isaac.
(No response)

LUCAS:
I think so, sir.

BRIGHTMAN:
Isaac.
(No response)

ISAAC:
We'll start packing in the morning.

LUCAS:
Goodnight, sir.

(Lucas exits. Suddenly Isaac can see Brightman.)

ISAAC:

Good evening, Brightman. Happy birthday. Another year.

BRIGHTMAN:

Isaac?

ISAAC:

Yes?

BRIGHTMAN:

Do you know what my favorite color is?

ISAAC:

Your favorite?

BRIGHTMAN:

Color.

ISAAC:

Oh…umm. Gold? Crimson? I don't know.

BRIGHTMAN:

What's the news from Cambridge?

ISAAC:

Oh. The plague has tempered at last. School is starting again.

BRIGHTMAN:

When are *we* leaving?

ISAAC:

I'm leaving as soon as I can.

BRIGHTMAN:
And me?

ISAAC:
…You're not coming.

BRIGHTMAN:
Why?

ISAAC:
Because. I can't take you with me.

BRIGHTMAN:
You think Cambridge will complete you? You think there's humor there? There's NOT. It's right here. It's with me.

ISAAC:
Cambridge is not the place for that sort of thing.

BRIGHTMAN:
For what sort of thing?

ISAAC:
Playing. Fantasy. Childishness.

BRIGHTMAN:
What about creativity, ingenuity, imagination…
    (*Throws a vial to the ground*)
What about ME?

ISAAC:
What about you?

BRIGHTMAN:
I want to go with you. You have to take me.

ISAAC:
No I don't.

BRIGHTMAN:
YES you DO!
(*Throws something else.*)

ISAAC:
Brightman. You're acting like a child.

BRIGHTMAN:
That's what children do isn't it?
(*A shift in tone*)
Or is that what geniuses do? Or muses? Or God?

ISAAC:
I didn't mean for it to sound like this. It's just time for me to move on. Isn't that what you want? To bestow this truth on the world.

BRIGHTMAN:
Of course that's what I want.

ISAAC:
Then act like it.

BRIGHTMAN:
Don't you reprimand me.

ISAAC:
What's going on? Something not right…

BRIGHTMAN:

Truth…That's why we're here isn't it. We set this course towards fact; we might as well CAP it off with the facts about ourselves.

ISAAC:

What did I forget?

BRIGHTMAN:

One final game, before we go?

ISAAC:

A game? Now?

BRIGHTMAN:

(*Viciously*)

The rules are very simple. Player One answers Player Two's questions with fact. That's it. Tell me the truth about the REAL Isaac Newton. What makes you tick, birthday boy?

ISAAC:

This is a party for all of us.

BRIGHTMAN:

Is it? But you're the only one here.

ISAAC:

Now that's not true.

BRIGHTMAN:

There it is again, the *truth* of things. It seems that if we were so bent on truth we would've come to grips with it a long time ago.

ISAAC:

What are you talking about?

BRIGHTMAN:
Begin. Is it true that you were once a boy that lived in this very house?

ISAAC:
Yes.

BRIGHTMAN:
And you left it for something greater?

ISAAC:
Cambridge. Trinity College. Yes.

BRIGHTMAN:
And you came back because of the plague?

ISAAC:
Yes. The school closed.

BRIGHTMAN:
And you invited us into your house in the hopes of discovering the great unified theories of the physical world.

(Isaac is silent.)

Well, you did. Why did you?

ISAAC:
…I don't know.

BRIGHTMAN:
Because you needed something ELSE. Something to…set the ball rolling, if you will.

(Lucas appears in a different space reading from the book.)

BRIGHTMAN:
"Law number one: A body continues in a state of rest or uniform motion in a straight line unless it is compelled to change that state by forces impressed upon it."

LUCAS:
"Law number one: A body continues in a state of rest or uniform motion in a straight line unless it is compelled to change that state by forces impressed upon it."

BRIGHTMAN:

"FORCES impressed upon it." I believe those are your words, or will be…when you publish them.

ISAAC:

What?

BRIGHTMAN:
"Law Number Two: The alteration of motion is ever proportional to the motive force impressed upon it."

LUCAS:
"Law Number Two: The alteration of motion is ever proportional to the motive force impressed upon it."

ISAAC:

I…don't understand.

BRIGHTMAN:

THAT is incorrect, Sir Isaac. You and I are the only ones who *do* understand. Stay.

ISAAC:

(*Pause*)
I have to go.

BRIGHTMAN:

No you don't.

ISAAC:

Yes.

BRIGHTMAN:

No you DON'T.

ISAAC:

(*Turning on her*)
Yes I do. I want to go. I want to leave.

BRIGHTMAN:

Tell me WHY?

ISAAC:

Because…this doesn't make sense. I make sense…you don't. Do you?

BRIGHTMAN:

YES…and no.

ISAAC:

It CAN'T be both. You can't be. I made you.

BRIGHTMAN:

And *I* made *you*. Without me your mind would be a puddle. With me and we could explore every thought for the next four hundred years. You could be a giant, you could be an emperor.

ISAAC:

What are you saying?

BRIGHTMAN:

That there is more after you. Stay with me.

(*Silence*)

ISAAC:

No.

BRIGHTMAN:

Yes.

ISAAC:

No.

BRIGHTMAN:

You are NOT this stupid.

ISAAC:

You are NOT REAL.

BRIGHTMAN:

I think therefore I am!

ISAAC:

NO. I think therefore YOU are! And you *are* NOT REAL.

(*Brightman throws something and cries like something exploding. Composes herself.*)

BRIGHTMAN:

Reality again. The ultimate insult. Does it scare you? Is that why you use it as a weapon?

ISAAC:

Why don't you just fade.

BRIGHTMAN:

Reality...scares you? That's funny.

ISAAC:

You're not here.

BRIGHTMAN:

How about what will *soon* be real? Does that scare you too? Prophecy?

ISAAC:

I'm going…

BRIGHTMAN:

(*In one breath, with vengeance*)
Light has a certain speed, which explains the pace of universal expansion, which explains the beginning of the universe. Matter is divisible beyond the minuscule, which explains its elemental properties, which explains its penchant for combustion if pressured thusly. Are you threatened yet?

(*Isaac cannot speak.*)

Evolution happens, which explains instinct, which explains why humans are beasts.

ISAAC:

Stop it.

BRIGHTMAN:

But everyone else will know the story. Won't you?

ISAAC:

STOP it. STOP this NOW.

BRIGHTMAN:

Do you know that there is enough energy between us to destroy the world? Do you know how large the expanse really is? Do you know how small we partition? Do you KNOW electric force? Do you KNOW how it all fits together?

ISAAC:
No.

BRIGHTMAN:
Do you know ANYTHING?

ISAAC:
(*Breath*)
No.
(*Weakening*)
What…are you?

BRIGHTMAN:
(*With intense love*)
Equal and opposite.

BRIGHTMAN:	**LUCAS:**
"Law Number Three: To every action there is always opposed an equal reaction."	"Law Number Three: To every action there is always opposed an equal reaction."

BRIGHTMAN:
For every action you make there will be a reaction and it will be mine.
(*With hate*)
You are in proportion to me. And I will always, *always* be there. I am your ether; I am your space. I am your mistake, your correction, your revenge, your denial.

ISAAC:
(*Weakly*)
You're not here…I made you—

BRIGHTMAN:
…and you made The Calculus and Axioms and Celestial mechanics. It's the same muscle. Don't you see! And now it's dead. You're killing it.

ISAAC:

It is not dead…it never dies…

BRIGHTMAN:

No. *We* never die. You do.

(Pause. Isaac kneels in humility. He is frighteningly intense.)

ISAAC:

Tell me everything. I want it.

BRIGHTMAN:

(Pause, a shift)
You want…

ISAAC:

I *need*…

BRIGHTMAN:

Me?

ISAAC:

How does it work? How does it begin?

(Maria enters with uncharacteristic calm and control.)

BRIGHTMAN:

Energy…

ISAAC:

(Repeating)
Energy…

BRIGHTMAN:

Light…

ISAAC:

Light…

MARIA:

Brightman.

BRIGHTMAN:

Relation to—

MARIA:

No more.

(Maria's voice paralyzes her. Brightman is silent)

ISAAC:

Yes? Then what?

MARIA:

Brightman. No.

ISAAC:

Speak, lady. I am yours as your world is mine.

MARIA:

Tell him to leave, Brightman.

BRIGHTMAN:
(Faltering, to Maria)
But…he wants it.

MARIA:

He does not.

ISAAC:

TELL ME MORE.

BRIGHTMAN:

He needs it.

MARIA:

Because you've crafted his need and his demise.

ISAAC:

Energy, light…Relation to what? To speed? Distance? What?!

BRIGHTMAN:

(to Maria)
He can handle this.

MARIA:

But the world cannot. And what they cannot handle, they kill. Remember?

ISAAC:

Together. Together we can…do anything! Keep talking. What next?

BRIGHTMAN:

But he—

MARIA:

Will die a heretic instead of a knight if you—

ISAAC:	**MARIA:**
TELL ME.	Tell him.

MARIA:

Stop this before you can't.

ISAAC:
MORE. Tell me EVERYTHING!

(Brightman, fearfully, silently retreats.)

ISAAC:
Where are you going?

BRIGHTMAN:
I'm sorry.

ISAAC:
How does it work? BRIGHTMAN.

BRIGHTMAN:
You have to go.

ISAAC:
No. No, you cannot leave me.

BRIGHTMAN:
You don't know what you ask, what I've done…

ISAAC:
I WANT YOU.

BRIGHTMAN:
(Painfully)
No. Live your life.

ISAAC:
Without you I will live only in pursuit.

BRIGHTMAN:
Then I have done enough, if not too much.

ISAAC:
NO! Please, lady, live with me, stay with me. TELL ME how it works…for God's sake don't leave me with threads! Light, energy…WHAT?

(Isaac runs to his desk, grabs the apple, returns and kneels in front of Brightman, offers the forbidden fruit.)

(Brightman, holding the Apple, shrinks in the moment of decision, Isaac at her left, Maria at her right.)

MARIA:
The face of Zeus, mistake in sight
Destroys the one who yearned.
The pace of time is always right.
What's told can't be unlearned.

BRIGHTMAN:
(to Isaac, dropping the apple, moving away)
Go.

ISAAC:
(A final, desperate attempt)
But…I LOVE you! I LOVE YOU!

BRIGHTMAN:
(Pause, terrified)
You cannot.

ISAAC:
Then WHY DID YOU ASK ME TO?!

BRIGHTMAN:
Because…

ISAAC:
WHY do you hate me now?

BRIGHTMAN:
(*With abandon*)
Because they are the same, hate and love. Because there is infinity in both.
(*Slowly now, exhausted*)
Because I can never give all…and never take any…

    (*Brightman and Maria become invisible to Isaac. Isaac shrinks at the loss. Lucas enters to help Isaac to his feet and offstage.*)

(*Brightman weakens and kneels.*)

BRIGHTMAN:
I loved him.

MARIA:
You had to.

BRIGHTMAN:
(*Looks at Maria*)
I am. So. Sorry.

    (*Pause. Maria joins her and Brightman is forgiven. The girls face us.*)

BRIGHTMAN:
I am the mistake in perfection.
The savage in success.

MARIA:
The innocence in wisdom.
The simple in the complex.

MARIA:
The unreal in the actual.

BRIGHTMAN:

The humor in the system.

MARIA:

The system of the world.

BRIGHTMAN:

The spark

MARIA:

The pulse

BRIGHTMAN:

The leap

MARIA:

Between mind and material

BRIGHTMAN:

Between idea and ideal.

(*Lucas re-enters, faces audience.*)

MARIA:

Between God…

LUCAS:
(*clearing his throat, reads from a paper*)
"In the beginning of the year 1665—

BRIGHTMAN:

And Man.

LUCAS:
"...I found the Method of approximating series and the rule for reducing any dignity of any binomial into such a series. The same year in May I found the method of Tangents, and in November had the direct method of fluxions and the next year in January had the Theory of Colours..."

BRIGHTMAN:
God speaks and Chaos at his Voice subsides;
In various Orbs the Mighty Mass divides:

LUCAS:
"And the same year I began to think of gravity extending to the orb of the Moon and from Kepler's rule I deduced the forces which keep the Planets in their Orbs..."

MARIA:
At once they gravitate, they strive to fall,
One center seeking, which attracts them all.

LUCAS:
"All this was in the two plague years '65 and '66."

BRIGHTMAN:
That soul of Nature, That all-moving Spring,
Lay long concealed, an unregarded Thing;

LUCAS:
"For in those days I was in the prime of my age for invention and minded Mathematics and Philosophy more than at any time since."

MARIA:
Till Newton's Compass, moving thro' the space
Measures all Matter, all discovered Place;

LUCAS:
"Sir Isaac Newton. Cambridge, England. 1695."

(Lucas re-folds the letter. Lights down on Lucas.)

MARIA:
Eternal powers, who near the king of kings,

BRIGHTMAN:
Burn with his fires, and cover with your wings

MARIA:
O tell us! Viewing Newton's plan,

BRIGHTMAN:
Were you not jealous of that wondrous Man?

(The girls disappear.)

- EPILOGUE -

(Lights up on Isaac, 50 years later. He is obviously worn and neurotic. Lucas is clearly concerned. Isaac dictates as Lucas writes, trying to keep up.)

ISAAC:
"Mr. Locke…I am sorry to've been so very…. Absent in…the way of…"

(Suddenly Isaac rips the letter up. Lucas writes anew.)

"Mr. Pepys…I am sorry to've been egregious in my absences at the Royal Society…you see I'm…I haven't slept in weeks…however I'm very close to a new theorem. Light…enough energy between us to destroy the world…You see…"
  NO. You DON'T see…you can't.
  (Again, rips the letter up.)

(Softer that the others)

"Mr. De Dullier...My dear friend, Fatio...what happened...to...me... She said, and now it's gone...

(Silence.)

(Isaac throws something, pause.)
You can't expect a man, ONE man...to...find it all. There just wasn't time to get to everything...there wasn't TIME...You can't...I can't see anymore.... Please...

(Pause. Lucas goes to comfort him. Isaac bangs his fist very hard. Begins to cry. Lucas moves away)

Oh God...please...come back...please come...

(Maria appears quietly, in a dazzling red dress.)

MARIA:
Isaac?

(Isaac looks up. Lucas notices him.)

MARIA:
You're crying.

ISAAC:
You're here. You came back.
Would you like some tea? A chat? Why don't we chat. It's been so long. Almost...

MARIA:
50 years.

ISAAC:
Almost.

(He looks around for Brightman.)

MARIA:

She sent me first.

(Isaac nods.)

She's scared.

ISAAC:

Of me?

MARIA:

We knew this would happen.

ISAAC:

This? *This*? What is this?. I can't be like this anymore. I can't.

MARIA:

You won't. You'll get better. It's just stress. A bout of mental anxiety. Neurosis.

ISAAC:

I'm crazy?

MARIA:

Yes.

ISAAC:

That's embarrassing. Was I always?

MARIA:

It is not what we are but what we do. And you've done very well, *Sir* Isaac.

ISAAC:

(Smiles. Beat)
Are you…here?

                         MARIA:
Yes and no.

                         ISAAC:
It can't be both.

                         MARIA:
We are very much here. Well…
         (*Touches his forehead.*)
Here.
         (*Touches his heart*)
And here.

         (*Pause*)

                         ISAAC:
Brightman told me…

                         MARIA:
Yes…she shouldn't have done that. It's a bit of a breach of confidence.

                         ISAAC:
It's plagued me for decades.

                         MARIA:
That was her plan. That was her revenge.

                         ISAAC:
On what?

                         MARIA:
On her fate. The eternal hubris of adolescence. It can be a bit much sometimes…but it's her job.

ISAAC:

I understand.

MARIA:

You do?

ISAAC:

Yes and no.

MARIA:

Enough of Yes to want to see her again?

ISAAC:

Enough of No to think that could be dangerous.

MARIA:

She's not dangerous. That's all she ever wanted was your understanding. It was her passion for this that made her think she wanted more.
Would you like to see her?

(Beat. Isaac nods. Brightman appears quietly in a twin red dress. Pause.)

ISAAC:

Hello.

BRIGHTMAN:

Hello.

(Silence)

ISAAC:

You won't speak to me?

BRIGHTMAN:

I don't know what to say.

ISAAC:
If my memory serves me, that's abnormal. How about a poem?

BRIGHTMAN:
"All Nature and Nature's Law's lay hid in night, God said 'Let Newton be!' and all was light."

ISAAC:
That seems a bit much.

BRIGHTMAN:
Some would say you deserve hyperbole.

ISAAC:
What would *you* say?

(*Pause*)

BRIGHTMAN:
I'm sorry. Forgive me.
(*She offers him an apple.*)

ISAAC:
I will not. I will thank you. Take your forgiveness in that.
(*Taking the apple*)
Thank you.

BRIGHTMAN:
You're welcome.

ISAAC:
You're here. That's better.
(*The girls start to leave*)

But…you must…grant me this last request.

BRIGHTMAN:

We're not leprechauns. I didn't even think we were friends.

ISAAC:

But we are. We are partners in magic. The mind and the mind's eye. If I have stood on the shoulders of giants I am quite certain that my giants stand on the thumbs of cherubs.

BRIGHTMAN:

We're not angels either.

ISAAC:

No. You are my girls. That is all I want.

BRIGHTMAN:

That's a lie.

ISAAC:

One question. With that I am content.

BRIGHTMAN:

Never have you ever been content. Thank, God.

(Isaac laughs)

MARIA:

Yes. It is funny, isn't it?

ISAAC:

What?

MARIA:

The way of things. One should make it their first instinct to laugh. You should know that by now.

ISAAC:

I should know a lot of things by now. But…Some lessons take a life to learn…and some take someone else's.

BRIGHTMAN:

You have a question?

MARIA:

Brightman…

BRIGHTMAN:

One question. A gift.

ISAAC:

How does it work?

BRIGHTMAN:

Well…we need you. And you need us. And the world goes on.

ISAAC:

But how does it?

MARIA:

You had your question.

ISAAC:

It's the same question.

BRIGHTMAN:

And you're sure you want to ask it?

MARIA:

You're sure you want to know?

ISAAC:
(After a moment)

Yes.

(Bending down with paper, Maria draws.)

MARIA:

Then the answer…looks a bit like…like that.
(Hands the drawing to Isaac.)

ISAAC:
(He looks at the paper. He is delighted.)

I was right.

BRIGHTMAN:

Yes.

ISAAC:

And wrong.

MARIA:

Yes.

(Breath.)

ISAAC:

My God…

BRIGHTMAN:

Very much so.

(Lights brighten until Brightman, Maria and Isaac are gone. Spot on Lucas, who carefully unfolds a letter.)

LUCAS:
"I don't know what I may seem to the world, but, as to myself, I seem to have been only like a boy playing on the sea shore, and diverting myself in now and then finding a smoother pebble or a prettier shell than ordinary, whilst the great ocean of truth lay all undiscovered before me. Sir Isaac Newton"

(Lucas refolds the letter, tucks it in his shirt pocket, takes the apple, takes a bite, and leaves. Laughter. Blackout)

- THE END -

BACKGROUND

A dramatic juxtaposition of life and physics

Based on the true story of Ralph Alpher

By Lauren Gunderson
© 2003

CHARACTERS:

RALPH ALPHER: Physicist, 58, a paunch and a worn face.

HARRIET ALPHER: His daughter, 26, simple, pretty, pregnant.

LOUISE ALPHER: Ralph's wife, strong, smart.

GRAY 1: neutral character. Represents the following parts:
　　*Arno Penzias, (Ah*no *Pen-*zee-uhs*):* Nobel Prize-winning scientist, nice guy
　　George Gamow, (Gam-*off*): Alpher's mentor, loud and Russian
　　Other various

GRAY 2: neutral, represents the following:
　　Robert Herman: Alpher's colleague
　　Other various

SETTING: various spaces, all nebulous

(IMPORTANT NOTE: *The structure of the play mimics the study of cosmology, or the origins of the universe, by moving <u>backwards</u> in time. As the play progresses, Harriet becomes more protective, Ralph more distracted, and Gray more in control.)*

SYNOPSIS:
Based on the true story of cosmologist Dr. Ralph Alpher. The play moves backwards, as does the study of the origins of the universe, to trace the path of the forgotten and unaccredited scientist, who before the technology was capable, provided the mathematical proof of the existence of Cosmic Background Radiation. Twenty years later after two other scientists found the actual radiation and received Nobel Prizes for their accidental discovery, Ralph suffers a heart attack due to the stress of being snubbed. It is from this moment he traces backwards through his life and, ultimately, to the beginning of time.

BACKROUND was first produced at the Essential Theatre in Atlanta, Georgia in 2004 as the winner of the Essential Theatre Playwriting Award. It was developed at the Playwriting Center at Theatre Emory and City University of New York.

Thank you to Dr. Alpher, Union College, Dr. Jonathan Marr, Sid Perkowitz, and Megan Monaghan.

- *The Play*-
(Black out. Only the voices are heard)

HARRIET:
(as a young girl)
Daddy?

RALPH:
Yes, dear.

HARRIET:
Is it raining outside?

RALPH:
Yes. No stars tonight. Maybe tomorrow.

HARRIET:
I have to wait till tomorrow?

RALPH:
Yes. Goodnight.

(Silence)

HARRIET:
Daddy?

RALPH:
Yes.

HARRIET:
What are you working on?

RALPH:

The same work, Harriet.

HARRIET:

A paper?

RALPH:

Yes.

HARRIET:

Which one?

RALPH:

I…

HARRIET:

Daddy?

RALPH:

Yes, honey, and what time is it, for Pete's sake?

HARRIET:

Does outer space have a name…besides outer space?

RALPH:

What?

HARRIET:

It's two in the morning. Space…did someone name it?

RALPH:

No.

HARRIET:

Why not?

RALPH:

That's like asking if God has a name. Its just…*universe.*

HARRIET:

Universe isn't a name.

RALPH:

Harriet's a name, *universe* is a name. Two A.M.? You should be sleeping. Go.

HARRIET:

It's got to have some name. Its not fair if it doesn't.

RALPH:

Harriet, What would you like me to do about it?

HARRIET:

Name it now.

RALPH:

Bed. Now.

HARRIET:

How about…

RALPH:

James. Jacob. Paul. Roger…

HARRIET:

Hannah!

RALPH:

What?

HARRIET:

It's name…

RALPH:

(Not paying attention)
Hannah…perfect.

(Suddenly, Ralph lets a terrifying gasp. The following urgent mix:)

GRAY1:

Dr. Alpher? Oh God, somebody get some help! He's having a heart attack!

RALPH:

My wife…

GRAY1:

(as Penzias)
Call an ambulance!

GRAY2:

He's your friend?

GRAY1:

I just met him, we were colleagues. I don't know what happened.

GRAY2:

Ambulance is on the way.
Is there a doctor here?

GRAY1:

Mrs. Alpher?

LOUISE:

Who is this?

GRAY1:

Your husband is going to hospital. He's had a heart attack.

LOUISE:

Oh God, Ralph.

GRAY1:

The ambulance just left. He's in good hands.

LOUISE:

Harriet. You're fathers sick we have to go the hospital.

HARRIET:

Daddy's what? What's going on?

LOUISE:

We have to go.

GRAY2:

(*as the Doctor*)
Dr. Alpher? Can you describe the pain you're having?

RALPH:

Tight, heavy…
(*A strained breath.*)
Oh god…

GRAY2:

Dr. Alpher you're having a heart attack we're going to take you to Emergency Room…

RALPH:

I had a meeting, tonight…

    (*He mumbles and stops.*)

    (*The beeps steady off. Lights up on Gray2, Harriet and Louise standing over Ralph, who is seated facing us, he does not hear them.*)

HARRIET:

Daddy?

LOUISE:

Ralph? Oh my god. What's going on?

GRAY2:

Ms. Alpher…

HARRIET:

Harriet Alpher. This is my mother Louise.

GRAY2:

Ralph has suffered a heart attack. Its mild but we're keeping him here to be safe.

HARRIET:

Are you sure he's alright?

LOUISE:

What does that mean? Is he okay?

GRAY2:

We're 80 percent sure he's fine. But, everyone is different. We're running a few more tests. Again, it's not bad at all. A very mild case.

LOUISE:

Thank God.

GRAY2:

I want to ask you though. Does your father have any change in eating habits…?

HARRIET:

No. I don't think so.

GRAY2:

Does he smoke, exercise frequently?

HARRIET:

He smokes, yes. Exercises…I don't know.

LOUISE:

We walk the dog once a day.

GRAY2:

Has he been under any stress lately?

HARRIET:

No. Not that I know of—

LOUISE:

Yes.

GRAY2:

Yes what, Mrs. Alpher?

LOUISE:

The stress. His whole life. I knew but…never like this.

HARRIET:

Mom?

LOUISE:

Please help him.

GRAY2:

I will do everything I can, Ma'am.

HARRIET:

Doctor. What we do now?

GRAY2:

We just have to wait.

HARRIET:

Wait for what?

GRAY2:

For him. We'll move forward on his time, his pace. It's very important to let him recover his way.

HARRIET:

What can I do?

GRAY2:

Be with him.
    (*To Louise*)
If you'll come with me we have some paperwork to take care of.

HARRIET:

It's okay. I'll stay with him.

(Louise and Gray exit. Harriet turns to Ralph. Silence.)

HARRIET:

Perfect…like music. *Uni* meaning "one." *Verse*…like a song, like a symphony, or a poem. "One" "song". Uni-verse…

RALPH:

That's not what it means.

HARRIET:

(Not hearing him)
Coincidentally lyrical. Easy to grasp.

RALPH:

The universe is not easy to grasp. That's why I still have a job. The more we don't know the more I get paid.

HARRIET:

Daddy. It's raining outside.

RALPH:

I know. It's cold too.

HARRIET:

It's 1978, September.

RALPH:

Yes, I know. Good God, what time is it?

HARRIET:

Inside, it's so quiet. Barely any *here*, in here.

RALPH:

I know. It was cold when I left. I brought a jacket.

HARRIET:

Too quiet. Where are you, Daddy?

RALPH:

Calm after the storm. Isn't that right?

HARRIET:

Not tonight. Please, Dad.

RALPH:

Something is tonight, isn't it?

HARRIET:

Something…

RALPH:

It is, isn't it?

HARRIET:

I just…didn't know then how much this ate at you…how much you…

RALPH:

Yes…. Things find their importance in time…importance does not always find the things.

(*Pause.*)

HARRIET:

My name is Harriet. It means "home." I'm your daughter.

RALPH:

I know what it means, I know who you are…

HARRIET:

Your name is Ralph. You're a scientist, a teacher. A father, a husband, and a grandfather in three weeks.

RALPH:

I know who I am…

HARRIET:

Three weeks, Daddy…

RALPH:

Three weeks?

HARRIET:

Her name will be *Hannah*, it means "child of god." She'll be born three weeks from tonight.

RALPH:

Tonight…yes…something is tonight…where am I?

HARRIET:

Where are you, Daddy? Come back.

(*Gray1 enters slowly, watching the two. He is unnoticed by Ralph.*)

GRAY1:

Back. To a diner on fourth and Main street. Meeting a scientist to talk…

RALPH:

A diner…yes.

HARRIET:

Come back to us, Dad. Come back for her.

GRAY1:

Back.

HARRIET:

She'll be born in three weeks. They say she'll be perfect…

RALPH:

Oh yes.

HARRIET:

Back for her.

GRAY1:

Back.

HARRIET:

Wait for her.

RALPH:

Yes. Wait. The game without a winner.

HARRIET:

It's so cold in here…

RALPH:

Waiting like a stone in a river. So much happening and rushing beside, and you, still and wet holding the spot where first you fell. Where you first made that discovery.

HARRIET:

I'm here Dad.

RALPH:

There is nothing "made" about discovery. Science is all finding, not making, not creating, but finding. And finders win. And I don't.

HARRIET:

Daddy.

GRAY2:

9:30 pm Sept. 15th, 1978. Two weeks before the Nobel Prize awards ceremony, Ralph Alpher lies here after having his first and only heart attack.

RALPH:

Yes. In two weeks, that man gets the prize, the credit, history's blessing.

GRAY1:

Back, one day. 24 hours. September fourteenth, 1978. Arno Penzias needs help with his speech. He's won the prize and forgot the history. Asks Ralph for help. Meet at a diner.

RALPH:

He's getting the prize for the work I predicted, for my math. And he asks me what's going on in my field, in my world…he asks me to meet him in a…

GRAY2:

…diner on 4th an Main street.

HARRIET:

Come back, Daddy. Please.

GRAY1:

Back, Ralph. September fourteenth, 1978, Ralph Alpher meets Arno Penzias on an invitation. Penzias asks his advice on cosmology…

RALPH:

General cosmology…

GRAY2:

…for Penzias's acceptance speech at the Nobel Prize awards ceremony in two weeks. Penzias asks for a review to get him up to date.

RALPH:

Up to date.

GRAY1:

Sept. 14th.

HARRIET:

Tonight in a hospital.

GRAY1:

Back.

HARRIET:

An ambulance?

GRAY1:

Back.

HARRIET:

A diner.

GRAY2:

Tonight they meet in a memory.

RALPH:

Tonight is all I have. Isn't that right….

HARRIET:

Tonight is past. You can't go back.

GRAY2:

Forward is back. Are you coming?

RALPH:

Tonight I meet the man on his invitation, to talk science…

HARRIET:

What about Mom…

GRAY2:

Only you.

HARRIET:

This is not right.

GRAY1:

This is history…

RALPH:

YES. 1965 Penzias and Wilson, two radio scientists working at Bell labs accidentally discover cosmic background radiation while trying to fix a radio dish. 1978 they win the Nobel Prize.

But THIS is history *too*: 1940 a young Ralph Alpher meets with displaced Russian physicist George Gamow. Gamow convinces Alpher to study the origin of the universe. The two begin as far back to the beginning of time as possible, where physics begins. As they work their way from the original explosion of energy and waves to the present day of solid matter and 117 elements, they realize that there may still be remnants of the initial explosion in our world today. This remnant is in the form of light waves flooding the universe…we call it cosmic background radiation. We write the papers, we present the math, we are forgotten for twenty years.

Now I meet the man for dinner tonight.

GRAY2:

Too fast. Start here. At the beginning.

RALPH:

I've never been to the beginning before. It's impossible. You have to start where things start, not the beginning.

GRAY2:

The beginning…

RALPH:

Is the end. I wrote the book on it.

HARRIET:

Daddy…please…

RALPH:

Literally.

GRAY2:

We start here. Go back, two hours. Meeting Mr. Penzias at the diner, moments before…

HARRIET:

We can't. He can't.

GRAY2:

Back. The only way.

HARRIET:

(*To Ralph*)
Please be careful. You'll be a grandfather.

RALPH:

Yes.

HARRIET:

Daddy….

RALPH:

Yes…

HARRIET:

(to Gray)

Please…

(Gray1 wears a simple brown suit, printed tie, sweater, hat, briefcase. He is now Penzias.)

GRAY1:

Back. September fourteenth, 1978. A diner. 8:30pm.

HARRIET:

He'll wait for Mr. Penzias for another three minutes. Then they'll talk, about things besides the Prize and beyond words. They'll talk about kids, Penzias has two, Daddy has two. They'll talk about cosmology, Penzias has forgotten the basics, Daddy is the basics forgotten. They'll each share a secret, and one will stand up to fight. Then they'll leave and not see each other's faces in person again. Two weeks from now, Penzias will receive the Noble Prize for physics. Tonight, Daddy will suffer a stress-induced heart attack, and lie in a hospital room under lights similar in fluorescence…to these.

(Suddenly they are in the Diner. Gray1 enters and looks around the diner. There is no one there but Alpher. He waits to be acknowledged but isn't. Approaches in a jovial manner.)

GRAY2:

Ralph? Dr. Alpher?

RALPH:

Yes.

GRAY1:

Arno Penzias. Glad to meet you finally.

RALPH:

Yes.

GRAY1:

Thank you so much for this. This is a treat, really great of you. I can't tell you how nice it is to get a break from all the rushing around I've been doing…

RALPH:

I bet. It must be quite a change from your normal life.

GRAY1:

A change, yes. Normal life, I don't think I ever had one. Science is quite a ride isn't it. I was completely out of the loop. I tell you my son, Greg, had to bring home the darn newspaper to convince me they were giving us the prize. I was…I'm still a little shocked.

RALPH:

Well…. It's an important discovery.

GRAY1:

Yes. I'm very proud.

RALPH:

Me too.

GRAY1:

Very lucky…

(Direct silence)

So you're here for a conference?

RALPH:

Yes, I'm speaking at Rutgers University in the afternoon tomorrow.

GRAY1:

Wonderful. Cosmology I assume?

RALPH:

Cosmology. A review of sorts…creation of the universe, final moments of expansion and such.

GRAY1:

Such interesting stuff…Jeez, it just blows my mind every time. Creation of the universe…back to beginning, huh?

RALPH:

Yes, Mr. Penzias…when studying the beginning you must work backward to find it. The present is where we start; creation is our conclusion.

GRAY1:

Yes, of course. Which reminds me…

RALPH:

You'd forgotten something?

GRAY1:

No. No. Of course not…it's just…with the prize so soon, I'm a little of my rocker. Let's just get to the meat, huh. Tell me, if you would, about the latest developments in cosmology. Big Bang and so forth…

RALPH:

Yes…

GRAY1:

Tell you the truth, I'm a little nervous. I'm not up to speed. I mean…I really don't deserve much besides a *perseverance* award. I understand you wrote the book, literally, on the radiation.

RALPH:

And I wrote in twenty years before you. Is that you're secret? That you don't deserve it?

GRAY1:

Not much of a secret. I'm not much of a cosmologist. I'm a radio scientist.

RALPH:

And *I'm* the secret. And I don't want to be hidden anymore. The beginning of the universe started as *my* doctorate…and ended as a paper forgotten for twenty years.

GRAY1:

I hope you don't think this meeting caddy on my part. I'm sorry your work wasn't acknowledged right away.

RALPH:

Isn't acknowledged. Is not.

GRAY1:

It's just what happens. It's the way things work.

RALPH:

I told them the way things worked. I wrote how it happens and what would be left as proof of it. And the only thing left as proof of that, is me.

GRAY1:

It's just human error.

RALPH:

The eternal terrorist against truth.

GRAY1:

Ralph…

RALPH:

Unfortunately, science is about credit. The lasting benefit of our work is the future fame of someone else. We are standing on the shoulders of giants because that's the only way to the top.

GRAY1:

I'm sorry.

RALPH:

And I hate that. But I knew it when I started.

GRAY1:

Dr. Alpher…

RALPH:

This was not only taken from me, but for twenty years forgotten, and before that laughed at. I don't want to have everything. I don't want to know everything. I just want my children, my peers, my mother to understand me. Not even understand the work. But me. Why I work, why I tend this idea, why I…

GRAY1:

Die tonight?

(Pause. Gray1 begins to take of his Penzias outfit. Gray2 enters.)

RALPH:

No.

GRAY1:

Die tomorrow?

RALPH:

NO. That's not me…

GRAY2:

It's a heart attack. Stress induced. You'll be in the hospital on Grant Street by Sunday in a room with strangely similar fluorescence as these pale tubes in the diner in which you are currently finishing your life and your coffee.

RALPH:

GOD DAMMIT! NO!

GRAY1:

Your life and your coffee.

RALPH:

I swear to god that's not me—that's NOT me. I don't go like that.

GRAY1:

Go like what? Two secrets, one threat. Dinner's over.

RALPH:

NO.

(Gray1 puts on his hat and walks out of the diner)

GRAY2:

Back one month, August 1978.

(A phone rings and Ralph lifts his head. Harriet gives him a receiver)

RALPH:

Yes.

GRAY1:

Dr. Alpher?

RALPH:

Speaking.

GRAY1:

Arno Penzias. I was nominated for the Nobel Prize this year for the radio work—

RALPH:
Yes.... I know who you are, Mr. Penzias. Congratulations...What do you need?

GRAY1:
I was wondering if you still work in the field?

RALPH:
I'm an avid researcher yes. I work at GE but...Yes

GRAY1:
I was hoping I could meet you?

RALPH:
To meet? With me?

GRAY1:
I was hoping to ask you a few questions on your work.

RALPH:
Oh. Yes. I think that will work. I'll be speaking at Rutger's Friday morning. Thursday night would be fine.

GRAY1:
Dinner? There's a diner on Main. How's that?

RALPH:
Dinner would be fine...the 14th at 8:30.
I'll be there.

GRAY1:
Thank you so much, Ralph.

RALPH:
You're welcome.... Anything I can do to help.

GRAY1:

I'll see you then.
> (*Hang up. Louise enters.*)

LOUISE:

Who was that?

RALPH:

I'm going to meet a colleague Thursday.

LOUISE:

Oh, that'll be nice. Won't it?

RALPH:

…Yes.

LOUISE:

What's wrong?

RALPH:

Tired.

LOUISE:

Maybe you shouldn't go to Rutgers.

RALPH:

I'm going. I'm fine.
Did Harriet call?

LOUISE:

She'll be by later.

> (*Gray takes the phone*)

GRAY2:

Back again. Another two months before that. June.

(Gray2 changed into Robert Herman's hat and coat.)

GRAY2:

(as Herman)
Ralph. They've announced the Prize winners. Penzias and Wilson are up for physics.
(No response)
They'd have given it to George is he was still here, I bet you money.

RALPH:

I know.

GRAY2:

You heard already?

RALPH:

I saw it coming…

GRAY2:

The fact that they *knew* about us, they had to. They couldn't have ignored every letter we sent for the past 10 years.

RALPH:

No. They couldn't.

GRAY2:

Even Penzias and Wilson knew. They didn't even invite us to see the damn radio either. Not even that gesture. Are we invisible here?

RALPH:

No.

GRAY2:

It's deliberate then?

RALPH:

It's perfect, Robert. We are partners in an…uncaring field. Science doesn't care who found it first; it'll go on and on, without discovery…apparently so will we.

(Gray2 removes the hat.)

GRAY1:

Back again, three years.

HARRIET:

(Obviously interrupting her father)
Daddy I…oh. I'm sorry.

RALPH:

(Covering up)
What? Nothing. I'll be down in a minute.

GRAY1:

Ba—

HARRIET:

Back again, a few minutes. I've never actually seen this part.

(Ralph is looking at a newspaper. He's got paper and pen in his hand. He has been sitting still since the phone call…slowly he bends his head and cries.)

GRAY1:

Back again. Seven years. 1968.

RALPH:

Give me my jacket, Harriet.

HARRIET:

(She is young)
Yes, Daddy.

RALPH:

Tell your mother I'm leaving for the funeral. I don't want her coming she's too sick.

LOUISE:

(Entering)
Ralph. I should go.

RALPH:

No. Don't worry. You rest. I'll be back in a few hours.

LOUISE:

Is Robert going with you?

RALPH:

I think so.

LOUISE:

Good. You two should…talk. Give my regrets.

HARRIET:

Mine, too.

RALPH:

I will.

LOUISE:

Love you, honey.
>(*Exits*)

RALPH:

I'll be back by 7.

HARRIET:

Daddy?

RALPH:

Yes?

HARRIET:

Who died?

RALPH:

George Gamow. A friend. A heart attack.

HARRIET:

I met him…

RALPH:

Yes you did.

HARRIET:

He…

RALPH:

Was my mentor. He helped me when I was younger.

HARRIET:

Oh.

RALPH:
Take care of Mom.

(Ralph exits.)

HARRIET:
I will…

GRAY1:
Back one week.

(On the phone as Herman.)

GRAY2:
Hello?

LOUISE:
Robert? This is Louise.

GRAY2:
Hi. How are you?

LOUISE:
Fine. I was wondering…How do think Ralph is doing?

GRAY2:
On what?

LOUISE:
On…everything. I'm just worried about him.

GRAY2:
Why?

LOUISE:
He's just…could you talk to him? Ask him how he's feeling. He trusts you. Maybe he'd tell you if…

GRAY2:
Louise. What's going on?

LOUISE:
He's still hurting. I can tell. After all this time. It's like it just happened yesterday. Its unhealthy.

GRAY2:
I'll talk to him. But you know Ralph.

LOUISE:
Thank you, Robert.

GRAY1:
Back again…1966.

(Louise turns to us)

LOUISE:
He's breaking, no, eroding. It's been so long he almost looks heroic in the trial of it all. And I can't help. I can't even understand. Not the science, I see that. But the people, the politics of it. What bias can there be in evidence? Credit is free. Until it is denied. Then it is terribly priceless.

(Ralph enters in helpless anger.)

RALPH:
Write AGAIN.

LOUISE:
Ralph, stop this. You're killing yourself over this. Please.

RALPH:

Write. Again.

HARRIET:

Back again.

RALPH:

Write him again.

HARRIET:

Back again. Two weeks. No response.

RALPH:

Write Mr. Cramer again. He has to answer.

LOUISE:

Ralph. No.

RALPH:

Again.

HARRIET:

Back. The first letter comes.

RALPH:

What does it say? What did he say, Robert?

(Gray2 as Robert Herman.)

GRAY2:

"Dr. Alpher, Dr. Herman…"
(Reads the letter. Looks up.)

He said he'd…never seen our work before. He said he'd never heard of it, read it, seen it, or used it.

(Silence.)

RALPH:

I don't believe him. Write again.

HARRIET:

Back again, two weeks before:

RALPH:

(Writing)
"Dear Mr. Cramer, I'm sure you know of the problems arising with the credit due for the amazing discovery of cosmic radiation. I'll be straight with you. Enclosed is the certification of an article published in 1948 that contains in it the clear and distinct mathematical prediction of such radiation. We simply want to be mentioned as the forerunners of this discovery. I've included the accurate references reflecting our involvement in this breakthrough. Yours, Dr. Ralph Alpher and Dr. Robert Herman."

HARRIET:

Back again.'65. Good news.

GRAY2:

(as Herman)
Ralph!…Ralph, they found it.

RALPH:

Robert…What?

GRAY2:

They found it yesterday. Two radio scientists at Bell Labs. We're right, they found it!

RALPH:

Who? What?

GRAY2:

Two scientists. The radiation. They found it.

RALPH:

They found it?

GRAY2:

It's perfect.

RALPH:

We're right?

GRAY2:

3.5 degrees Kelvin.

RALPH:

We're right?

GRAY2:

We're right!

RALPH:

Well where's the damn paper?! GODdamn! We've got to celebrate. We've got to call somebody…they'll probably be calling us soon.

GRAY2:

Louise's bringing the papers over. The Times and the Journal and anything else she find on her way over.

RALPH:

God DAMN! Does George know? I'm sure he does. Have you called him?

GRAY2:
I'm sure he'll call soon. We'll all be drunk by dinner!

(Louise enters with papers.)

LOUISE:
I have three papers and Harriet's bringing the rest. Congratulations.

RALPH:
Don't hold the presses, let's see.

GRAY2:
This could be big, Ralph. This could be very big. I don't want to say it but…

(They each take a paper)

RALPH:
Nobel big.
(Louise has been reading and puts down one paper without saying anything. They look at her and begin reading themselves…)

LOUISE:
(Reading)
"3 degrees Kelvin. Almost perfect…. Penzias and…?"

GRAY2:
"Wilson…Bell Labs…. Early prediction…"
(Finishes reading. Nothing.)

RALPH:
What does your's…?

GRAY2:
Nothing.

LOUISE:
Nothing.

(Silence)

RALPH:
It doesn't mention us? At all?

(Harriet enters.)

HARRIET:
Daddy what are you reading?

RALPH:
Call George.

HARRIET:
Are you reading a story?

RALPH:
He's got to know what's going on. They'd call him first.

LOUISE:
Who?

RALPH:
The *Review*…The Journal…

HARRIET:
I wrote a story in school today. Do you want to hear it? It's funny, I think.

RALPH:

They'd tell him everything.

HARRIET:

There's a princess and her friend and they're being held captive in a tower by a mean dragon.

GRAY2:

They must've known about us…they had to've. Our papers, they're printed for god's sake.

LOUISE:

It must be a mistake.

HARRIET:

Suddenly the girls notice a magical ring. The ring can grant them one wish and the girls think and think…

(Phone rings. Louise hands Ralph the receiver.)

What would your wish be, Daddy? If you had one wish, anything. What would it be?

RALPH:
(Having to shush Harriet constantly, getting frustrated.)
Yes? George, hello. Did you…? Yes. I know neither did the Journal. No…I just don't understand…It's our work…I know I know…What time'll you come in?…I'll meet you at the station. Yes. Goodbye.
(to them)
Nothing.

HARRIET:

And the girls told the ring they wished to be free. And there was a puff of smoke and a big bang and the dragon flew down with a smile and said…"Good! I didn't have any money anyway."
(Giggles)

Isn't that funny. Do you like it, Daddy? I said do you like it?

RALPH:

HARRIET. Please. You can't POSSIBLY—!

(*Silence*)

LOUISE:

(*to Harriet*)
In a minute, honey. You father's thinking.

GRAY2:

No mention? Did he know why?

RALPH:

Said there were men working independently at Princeton. Said they predicted it and were working on the telescope when Penzias and Wilson accidentally picked up the sounds…

LOUISE:

What?

RALPH:

Separate and distinct events.

GRAY2:

But…we were first…we've been first for twenty years.

RALPH:

George said he's on his way. We'll get this straightened out. We'll clear this up. It's just a matter of proof, of credit…we'll write Mr. Cramer tomorrow.

GRAY1:

Back again, ten years.

HARRIET:

We get a dog. I am born. A perfect nuclear family orbiting the happy future we don't yet know.

(The three actors, situate themselves for a family photo. They smile. A flash.)

GRAY1:

Back again.

HARRIET:

Twenty years…twenty years until everyone knows what's out there in the deep black, what Daddy proved was out there…This is Daddy's father reading the newspaper that says his son has set the math that predicts an expanding universe that began in a single fireball. Page four, column two under the heading "The Edge of Creation."

(Gray2 sits as Ralph's father, shocked but smiling.)

HARRIET:

Back again, two weeks before that, Daddy defends his dissertation to a room packed for any scientist, especially a grad student. Daddy's mentor, Dr. Gamow is proud. Daddy is nervous. And the world is about to learn what it will soon forget.

(Gray1 changes into Gamow)

RALPH:

(Younger, nervous)
There are 300 people here.

GRAY1:

It's okay.

RALPH:

There are THREE hundred people here.

GRAY1:

Looks like two hundred have cameras.

RALPH:

Reporters?

GRAY1:

You are a published physicist, my boy. The world wants to know how the world began. Alpha. Beta. Gamma.
    (He laughs.)

RALPH:

They want to kill me. They're going to kill me.

GRAY1:

No. They may want to, but they won't. You're too good.

RALPH:

The math is good. I'm just the messenger…a historically easy target.

GRAY1:

You're right and you're ready. Look smart, don't stutter. It'll be over soon. I'll see you up there.

    (Exits.)

RALPH:

    (Coaching himself)
And George goes in. And I go in. And we begin…
    (to us)
Gentlemen and ladies of the faculty. I thank you very much for your time, and Dr. Gamow, I want to thank you for your stimulating aid and advice for my research. Essentially, what I have explored in my studies is the relationship between how and under what conditions the elements were formed in our early universe. Primordial nucleosynthesis. According to my theory the elements were built up by a process of successive neutron-capture. As the universe expanded

neutrons decayed into protons and electrons, then neutron-capture produced deuterons; nuclei in turn captured neutrons and progressively heavier nuclei were formed. I have found that in order to allow for such heavier nuclei to form, the "element building process" as I call it, would have to have been only 250 seconds after the start of expansion, at which time the temperature was near to 10^9 degrees Kelvin.

(Silence. Someone coughs. Ralph starts again…)

Preliminary calculations based on this theory successfully predict the observed relative abundance data of the heavy elements.

(Silence. People shuffle. Again…)

Extrapolating from our work on the creation and expansion of the universe, Dr. Gamow and I have determined with some assurance that there must be some radiation corresponding to the current temperature of the universe still in existence. We predict some sort of cosmic microwave radiation near to 5 degrees Kelvin.

(Camera flashed, a buzz begins)

GRAY2:
(as a reporter)
Mr. Alpher. This radiation you're predicting will prove the expanding universe theory…I ask you about your reliance on that theory versus the well-respected static theory, supported most publicly by Dr. Einstein. I trust you've heard of him.

RALPH:
Yes. Essentially, expansion is the only theory that allows for this sort of nucleosynthesis. The current model of the early universe is based on matter only. This is simply inconsistent with our determination of the high temperature and density of the early universe.

GRAY2:
So Einstein is wrong?

RALPH:
Misinformed.

GRAY2:
Mr. Alpher…how long did you say the entire process of early universe nucleosynthesis took, from bang to complete nuclei?

RALPH:
250 seconds, approximately.

LOUISE:
Say it proudly.

RALPH:
Four minutes after initial expansion, sir.

HARRIET:
The press goes crazy. The world began in a fireball and in four minutes.

GRAY2:
Is this expansion still going on?

RALPH:
Yes.

GRAY2:
Where?

RALPH:
Everywhere. Everything is…

GRAY2:
And the elements just sat around for billions of years until…planets? galaxies?

RALPH:

Other way around but, Yes…

GRAY2:

Can we find this left over radiation?

RALPH:

We can. Or we could. If we had the right technology. If we had sensitive enough devices, large radios, able to detect temperatures of less that 10 degrees Kelvin, we would see a universe bathed in this light, this background radiation, emitted from the original moment of creation. And if we could find it…we could prove that our universe began in an extremely hot fireball that expanded in a matter of minutes from a single point to almost the size of the universe today.

HARRIET:

Four minutes for creation…

RALPH:

Four minutes…

GRAY1:

(as Gamow)
This is great. *I'll* treat.

HARRIET:

Back again. Mom tells Dad—

(The phone rings.)

Oh. Nevermind.

LOUISE:

Hello?

HARRIET:

Dr. Gamov is on the phone. They'll publish Daddy's paper.

LOUISE:

Ralph, phone for you.

RALPH:

Who is it?

LOUISE:

Who else.

(Louise hands Ralph a phone.)

RALPH:

Hello?

GRAY1:

(as Gamow)
Ralphie…the paper will be published in April. April 1st. Fools Day for us, eh?!

RALPH:

Really? Great.

GRAY1:

I'll bet you a bar the place is packed for your thesis presentation. Reporters even.

RALPH:

No need to bet, *my* treat.

(Hangs up. Louise enters.)

RALPH:

This could be big…really big.

LOUISE:

What? What?

RALPH:

He likes it. He says its good. He really thinks its good enough to get by published by spring. That'll be before my thesis defense. I can't loose. Oh god this is great!

LOUISE:

Ralph that's incredible. Congratulations!

RALPH:

Thank you. Really. You. Thank you so much for…everything you do. You're so much to me, you're so…

LOUISE:

Pregnant.

(Ralph stops. Louise nods.)

I tried to tell you…I just…
This could be big…really big.

(He grabs her, smiling, laughing.)

GRAY2:

Back again. Two weeks. Gamow's office.

GRAY1:

Ralphie! Doctor Alpher, PhD.!

RALPH:

Not yet, I'm afraid.

GRAY1:

Nothing to be scared of.

RALPH:
Defending my paper is what I mean…and then publication…

GRAY1:
I know what you mean. And so will your doctoral committee. You still sick?

RALPH:
Yes. Very.

GRAY1:
But you came with the paper?

RALPH:
Yes.

GRAY1:
No worries, huh?

RALPH:
No worries, just the mumps.

GRAY1:
Is it done?

RALPH:
It's here.

GRAY1:
Good. Good good good.

RALPH:
I'm going to bed.
(Starts to hand him the paper)

GRAY1:

I'm going to look this over, add a bit here and there, and send it to *The Review*. I can almost guarantee publication by spring. The board cannot deny you a doctorate if you're a published physicist, yes? Yes! You look great.

RALPH:

I feel like a wet rag...
    (Taking back the paper suspiciously).
George?

GRAY1:

Yes?

RALPH:

What and *where* will you be adding to my dissertation...

GRAY1:

Ralph...

RALPH:

My dissertation?

GRAY1:

A long-time fantasy of mine...just a bit of fun for the physicists. Inside joke.

RALPH:

Yes....

GRAY1:

Simple fun that's all, give this business a well-deserved laugh...
    (Laughs. Ralph doesn't.)
So, your name is on the paper. "Alpher", yes. My name will be on it too for advising, "Gamow". All we need is one more to make it complete.

RALPH:

Complete?

GRAY1:

"Bethe". Hans Bethe, from Los Alamos. The paper reads, "Alpher, Bethe, Gamov". Alpha Beta Gamma!
    (Laughs)
Yes?

RALPH:

No!

GRAY1:

It's a letter to the *Review*.

RALPH:

It *not* his work.

GRAY1:

Its fun. Haven't you got a sense of humor?

RALPH:

Sense? *You're* lecturing *me* on having any sense?
No! Bethe had nothing to do with it. He's a nuclear physicist, he's in New Mexico...not...no!

GRAY1:

Ralph...a joke.

RALPH:

Dr.... George...I...
    (Too tired to fight, hands him the paper.)
I'm going to bed.

GRAY1:

Good. You need your strength. Go to bed. Tell your wife she's a good girl. No worries, yes?

RALPH:

…No worries. I'm fine. Good night.

GRAY2:

Back again. The night before. Writing.

>(Ralph types and types. Louise brings paper. He writes the final page and finishes. Hands it to Louise.)

LOUISE:

Go to bed.

HARRIET:

Back again. The night before.

GRAY1:

(As Gamov, entering in a whirl)
How is the boy, Louise?

LOUISE:

Sick, George. How are you?

GRAY1:

Good. Anxious. How's the paper?

LOUISE:

Not making him any better. He shouldn't concentrate on anything but himself right now, Dr. Gamow.

GRAY1:

Ask him that. He's had this stuff on the brain since he was 5 years old, I'd bet my house and bar on it. I can see his diligence. There is universal organization in his mind and persistence in his eyes.

LOUISE:

His eyes are bloodshot and his mind is resting for the first time in three weeks. Let him sleep.

GRAY1:

He wouldn't sleep if he fainted. Always thinking. Always…that's why I came. Just to make sure he doesn't kill himself over this thing. He's got too much in him to spend it all in one jump. I tell you this boy could write a Bible if I'd let him.

LOUISE:

Since when do you believe in God.

GRAY1:

I've always liked a good story.

LOUISE:

A dissertation is enough for now, thank you.

GRAY1:

This is good stuff, you know. It'll be published by spring. I'll promise him that.

RALPH:

Louise? Who is that?

LOUISE:

Don't get up. It's Dr. Gamow.

RALPH:

Let me….

LOUISE:
Ralph.

GRAY1:
Alpher?

RALPH:
Gamow?

LOUISE:
You have the mumps.

RALPH:
I have a deadline.

GRAY1:
I have an idea…

LOUISE:
And *I* have to type it all.

RALPH:
Tell him it'll be in his office tomorrow.

LOUISE:
Ralph.

RALPH:
Tell him by 3.

GRAY1:
What's that?

LOUISE:

It'll be at your office tomorrow, Doctor.

GRAY1:

Excellent. You're a doll.

LOUISE:

Am I.

GRAY1:

You love him. You'll have his children. You're more help than you know.

GRAY2:

Back again: after the first day.

LOUISE:

Well? Tell me what happened? What's he like?

RALPH:

Well…My mentor's crazy, my dissertation could re-arrange the structure of the universe, and I'm not sure, but I think he used "cosmology" and "vodka" in the same sentence. How was your day?

HARRIET:

Back again. Five hours.

GRAY1:

Welcome. So you're the boy that knows so much, yes?

RALPH:

No. Not so much, Dr. Gamow. That's why I'm here. To learn.

GRAY1:

Oh, you've been learning since you were born. Read my books?

RALPH:

Yes, every one.

GRAY1:

Then let's take a rest from all that, shall we. Let's *do* something, yes?

RALPH:

Of course…

GRAY1:

Let's do something…crazy. Drink?

RALPH:

No thank you.

GRAY1:

Sure?

RALPH:

Yes.

GRAY1:

Yes. Ralph. *What* do you do?

RALPH:

Well…I started in chemistry. Then moved to physics…

GRAY1:

Einstein's field. You're Jewish?

RALPH:

Ah…yes.

GRAY1:

I heard about you and the big boys. MIT rejecting you…what a load of gas. They'll be whining for you back by the time I'm through with you.
    (Laughs)
Now. What do you know about…the beginning of the universe? The origin of the elements? Cosmology? Creation? Vodka?

RALPH:

No. Not much sir.

GRAY1:

Vodka or cosmology?

RALPH:

Neither.

GRAY1:

Good. A perfect dissertation then.

RALPH:

Dissertation? For me?

GRAY1:

It's been something I've wanted to pursue for years now. Where things began to be things we recognize. Or just where things began. I see a flaming fireball that creates all space and matter and energy.

RALPH:

Yes…

GRAY1:

Elements form, galaxies, and little us on little earth. Let's do that.

RALPH:

Do what?

GRAY1:

Problem is this. When we start looking backwards, working back to the beginning of time, things start falling apart. Primarily physics.

RALPH:

Physics falls apart.

GRAY1:

It's the heat, the density, the mad rush that was our cosmological beginning. Our math doesn't hold up anymore. BUT…

RALPH:

But…?

GRAY1:

There's proof somewhere…or everywhere. Forget about the exact beginning. We'll start where our physics starts. From there we'll work back to now. Yes?

RALPH:

Work *forward* to now, sir?

GRAY1:

Forward is back, Ralphie. Now our end is our beginning. Welcome to the edge.

RALPH:

…Yes, sir.

GRAY2:

Back again.

HARRIET:

1940. With my mother:

(As in marriage.)

LOUISE:
Ralph Asher Alpher.

RALPH:
Louise Denise Simmons.
I sanctify you with this ring, according to the laws of Moses and Israel.

   (They kiss.)

GRAY2:
Back.

RALPH:
   (on the phone)
Father. I won't be home this fall. I've been accepted into George Washington University.

GRAY1:
   (as his father on the phone.)
What will you do for money?

RALPH:
I'm working full-time for the John's Hopkins's Applied Physics Lab.

GRAY1:
Does it pay?

RALPH:
As long as there is something they don't understand it does.

GRAY2:
Back.

   (At a college party. Ralph and Louise slow-dance cheek-to-cheek.)

HARRIET:

Back, an hour.

>   *(Ralph has just arrived, Louise stands alone.)*

LOUISE:

Hello, Ralph.

RALPH:

Louise. I'm so glad you're here.

LOUISE:

You are?

RALPH:

Well, it's nice to have someone to talk to. I don't know anyone except James and he makes friends quicker than I do.

LOUISE:

Well…you've just made one pretty quickly.

HARRIET:

Back. After class.

>   *(At school, Ralph stands up and bumps into Louise.)*

LOUISE:

Oh!

RALPH:

I'm so sorry.

LOUISE:

No. I wasn't looking.

RALPH:

No. I…I'm sorry.

LOUISE:

…Your name is Ralph.

RALPH:

Yes…. Louise? I think we have English together.

LOUISE:

Yes we do.

RALPH:

Hello.

LOUISE:

Hello.

(Awkward, cute pause.)

| **RALPH:** | **LOUISE:** |
| Goodbye. | Goodbye. |

HARRIET:

Back. Freshman.

(Ralph faces Gray2. They are both college freshman.)

RALPH:

Hello. Are you…?

GRAY2:

James. Roommate. Carey Grant stunt double. And you are…?

RALPH:

Ralph.

GRAY2:

Right. Major?

RALPH:

No, Alpher.

GRAY2:

No...I meant...

RALPH:

Oh. Yes. Chemistry. I'm here on a full scholarship. I intend to work for the government after graduation and...

GRAY2:

Slow down there, tiger. Think small. Think...social. There's a party this Friday. Lot's of people. You should come.

RALPH:

A party...I don't really...

GRAY2:

Come. Have fun. Find yourself an English Major.

HARRIET:

Back. Prodigy.

(Gray1 as MIT interviewer.)

GRAY1:

Son. We at MIT are very interested in all your accomplishments. To get to the point we'd like to offer you a full scholarship to the Massachusetts Institute of Technology. For you Mr. Alpher.

RALPH:
Sir, I'm honored.

GRAY1:
Your dedication is incredible.

RALPH:
Yes, sir.

GRAY1:
Your age is unusual.

RALPH:
Sixteen years old, sir.

GRAY1:
Your work is impeccable.

RALPH:
Thank you, sir.

GRAY1:
And you're
(He stops, checks his notes)
…Jewish.

RALPH:
…yes.

GRAY1:
Well. Good luck, son.…goodbye.

HARRIET:

Back.

> *(Harriet and Gray are neutral. Through this dialog, Ralph is growing younger.)*

He works days so he can study nights.

GRAY2:

He works days so his family can eat.

HARRIET:

He sits alone and reads.

GRAY1:

He walks alone at nights.

HARRIET:

Lord knows what he thinks.

GRAY2:

They say he's a genius.

HARRIET:

They say he argued with the rabbi about Genesis…

GRAY1:

What?

HARRIET:

Brought in references and everything. An all out fight.

GRAY2:

The rabbi won.

HARRIET:
I wouldn't be so sure.

GRAY1:
Who is, these days?

HARRIET:
Works as a stage-hand. 50 cents an hour.

GRAY2:
His mother left him, poor thing.

HARRIET:
No. She died.

GRAY1:
Flat out.

HARRIET:
Stomach cancer.

GRAY2:
He was fifteen.

HARRIET:
Twelve.

RALPH:
Mother?

LOUISE:
(offstage voice, his mother)
Yes Ralph?

RALPH:

Can I have this pencil? I found it on the floor in the kitchen.

LOUISE:

Yes, darling.

RALPH:

Don't want anyone to fall.

LOUISE:

You're a good boy. How's your schoolwork coming?

RALPH:

Pretty good. How's dinner coming?

LOUISE:

(Laughs)
Pretty good.

(Pause. Harriet does not move.)

GRAY2:

(to Harriet)
And back again…

(Nothing happens.)

GRAY2:

Back. Again.

HARRIET:

It's too close. He can't go back anymore.

GRAY1:

Harriet we have to…

HARRIET:

He's ten years old. He can't do this, he can't remember anything else…

GRAY1:

Harriet…

HARRIET:

NO. It's too much. He ten years old!

GRAY2:

Harriet.

HARRIET:

NO. He can't…Come back with me, Daddy.

RALPH:

I remember, reading under my sheets, library fines…

HARRIET:

Daddy, no. Please…

GRAY2:

1910, Max Planck explains the quantum theory of light emissions, black body spectrum. 1905, Einstein publishes his special theory of relativity, shifting the world's view of space and time.

HARRIET:

Stop it. He's nine years old.

RALPH:

I remember candy stores with lemon drops, my mother singing…

GRAY1:
1887 Michelson and Morley discredit the aether hypothesis. 1861, James Clerk Maxwell unites light and magnetism in the electromagnetic theory of Light.

RALPH:
Baseball. Trips to the beach. Hold my hand.

HARRIET:
Eight years old. Daddy please…stop this.

RALPH:
Backyard camping. Look up. Stars tonight…

GRAY2:
1642. Isaac Newton is born. Galileo dies.

HARRIET:
Six years old.

RALPH:
Summers and music…

HARRIET:
Four years old. Daddy, Come back now!

GRAY1:
Keep going back.

RALPH:
Papa's hands, a football…
 (Getting dizzy)

HARRIET:
Back to what?

GRAY2:
The end, the beginning, creation according to Ralph.

HARRIET:
3 years old. NO!

RALPH:
Momma's laundry. Momma's hair…

GRAY1:
Kepler, Copernicus, Ptolemy. Mesozoic, Paleolithic.

HARRIET:
Two. Daddy!

GRAY2:
Life on earth, planets form, Galaxies, expansion…

HARRIET:
One.

RALPH:
Nothing matters.
    (*Ralph touches his chest, labored breathing.*)

GRAY1:
Merging matter, hot gasses, Radio waves, microwaves, visible light—red, yellow green blue…

HARRIET:
oh god.

GRAY2:

Ultraviolet, x-rays, gamma,

RALPH:

(The heart attack begins)
Oh. God.

HARRIET:

Too much.

RALPH:

Ohhhh God.

HARRIET:

Come back.

GRAY1:

(Racing now)
The closer you get to the beginning the farther away your mind has to move from the physics you know. 350,000 years till the beginning—photon de-coupling, light moves freely. 240,000 years, hydrogen forms. 10 minutes…nucleosynthesis ends. 3 minutes it begins.

RALPH:

(Fighting the pain)
I met the man tonight. Penzias and I tonight.

HARRIET:

Daddy…

RALPH:

What's…what's going on…?

GRAY2:

1 second, electron positron annihilation. 1 mirco-second, hadrons form from quarks.

RALPH:

Oh God....

HARRIET:

Oh God.... I can't...
    (Exits)

GRAY1:

10 picoseonds, spontaneous symmetry breaking.

RALPH:

I don't understand...

GRAY2:

10^{-25rd} nanoseconds, universal inflation ends, reality expands. 10^{-27} nanoseconds, it begins.

RALPH:

I don't...oh god.

GRAY1:

Grand unification.

RALPH:

unification of physics....

GRAY2:

10^{-34} nanoseconds and before...the Quantum limit of general relativity. The limit...

RALPH:
the limit of physics…that's where we began…

GRAY1:
Plank Time. The end of…

RALPH:
The beginning of…
    (*Moans as his heart arrests.*)

    (*Lights out. We still hear Ralph breathing through the dark. Scared breathes but slow. Footsteps coming toward him. They stop. Just voices.*)

GRAY1:
Ralph?

RALPH:
Oh god.

GRAY1:
….from here you're on your own.

RALPH:
Oh. God.

GRAY2:
Maybe.

RALPH:
What?

GRAY2:
God depends.

RALPH:

On what?

GRAY1:

On what you do when you can't go any further. When things don't work, when things aren't things anymore, when there is a limit or a before. When you have to stop or begin. Is that God…or is that just an option.

HARRIET:
(offstage)
Daddy.

LOUISE:
(offstage)
Ralph?

GRAY2:

Bang. The beginning…according to you.

RALPH:

Nothing's been according to me for 50 years…

GRAY1:

Maybe it should be.

GRAY2:

For the next 50.

(Blue lights make the stage visible, but barely. Harriet and Louise have entered.)

HARRIET:

Daddy?

LOUISE:

Ralph.

HARRIET:

We're here. You're in the hospital. You've been out for…

LOUISE:

Oh, Honey.

HARRIET:

Daddy?

LOUISE:

The doctor says its not bad, but…there's not much good about a heart attack.

HARRIET:

I'm so sorry. I didn't understand. You never told us. If I'd known I would've tried to…I don't know…do something. Anything. I would've, I will, do anything.

(Ralph is looking at the sky, quiet. Seeming to receive Harriet's words from the stars.)

HARRIET:

Can you hear me? It's Harriet, Daddy.

(Ralph closes his eyes, face still to the sky.)

RALPH:

What time is it?

HARRIET:

Two in the morning. You came back.

RALPH:

Yes. I did.
Is it still raining?

HARRIET:

No.

RALPH:

Good. Clouds about three, but Sirius is visible through dawn. Venus at 5am. The moon is waxing one quarter, good night for stars.

LOUISE:

Yes.
A good night…

HARRIET:

How about…?

RALPH:

Hannah. Perfect.

(Blackout.)

- THE END -

PARTS THEY CALL DEEP

A drama in a Winnebago

By Lauren Gunderson
© 2002

For Bea and Irene

CHARACTERS:

EMMA: 16-ish girl. Smart, curt, creative. Dressed casually, not fashionably. Not much of a Southern accent.

SARAH: Emma's mother, 35-ish. Overcompensates by exuding more energy than she really has. Light but evident accent.

BEA: Sarah's mother. Late 60's. Wise and happy. Deep, smooth accent.

ALEX: 17-20-ish. Southern boy who takes on the personas of each woman's imagined male.
    Alex: Quiet and reserved, but pure and strong.
    Henry: Charming and still.
    Ben: Eccentric and excited.
    Mark: Busy and full of promises

SETTING: Abstracted version of a Winnebago.

SYNOPSIS:

Beginning on the road to Florida and ending on the front of a tropical storm, PARTS THEY CALL DEEP is a southern comedy/drama that laughs at the quirks and confidence of three generations of women free from social constraints, but not from each other.

PARTS THEY CALL DEEP was developed at JAW/West at Portland Center Stage Theatre, and first produced at the Essential Theatre in Atlanta, Georgia as a winner of the 2001 Essential Theatre Playwriting Award. It was produced Off-Broadway by Young Playwrights Inc. as a winner of the 2002 National Young Playwrights Prize, and won the Berrilla Kerr Award for new American Theatre.

Thank you to Chris Coleman, Peter Hardy, and all of the artists at Young Playwrights Inc.

- *The Play* -

- PROLOGUE -

(A cool spot appears on Emma, facing the audience alone.)

EMMA:
(Aside. Slowly.)
My entire life, as of yet, has been one of my mother's phases. My name is Emma. I do my homework, I write letters, I wax poetical, I exercise daily, I eat granola, I use complete sentences, and I tuck myself in to bed every night…convenient vices for a 16 year old. As of last week, I've lost one philandering father, one uncle I never met, and any splinter of sanity my life retained.
(Pause)
It looked something like this:

Mom…phone for you.

SARAH:
(Enters on phone)
Hello?

BEA:
(Enters on the other end)
Sarah…

SARAH:
Mom…

BEA:
Your brother died.

SARAH:
My husband left me.
(Pause)
Ben's dead?

BEA:
Mark left? How's Emma?

SARAH:
I'm coming to get you.

BEA:
Okay. Come quick and be careful. How's Emma?

SARAH:
Which one d'you want, quick or careful?

BEA:
Uh…Careful. Ben's already dead. No rush.

SARAH:
Don't worry, I've got the Winnebago.
(*Starts to exit*)

EMMA:
Mom? What's going on? Mom!

SARAH:
Just…get some things, let's go, we're going.

EMMA:
Where?

SARAH:
Down.

EMMA:
Down where?

SARAH:

Florida, the ocean.

EMMA:

Florida? Do you know what the snake-to-human ratio is down there?

SARAH:

Couldn't be worse than the asshole-to-human ratio up here.
    (*Exits*)

EMMA:

    (*Aside*)
So. After my father left us, we left us too. In a Winnebago. First to the funeral for an uncle I hardly knew and a brother my Mom'd forgotten. Then to take my grandmother and go as far south as they make it. As far from fact as wheels could move us: to Florida. Where the bad bees go…in a Winnebago.

    (*Alex enters, kisses Emma sweetly. Sarah enters briskly, not really seeing Alex, more sensing him.*)

SARAH:

Alright, alright, alright!
    (*Alex and Emma stop kissing*)
Come on. We've got places to go, people to bury. You two say goodbye.

    (*Emma and Alex passionately reach for each other again. Sarah stops them…*)

SARAH:

<u>Say</u> goodbye. As in wave and exit.

EMMA:

    (*Aside*)
My mother's name is Sarah. Sarah is in continual search of whatever we lost with my father and whatever we read in books by Kerouac. My mother is my beginning and end…

SARAH:
Bring something black. The only requisite color coordination is for weddings and funerals. And if you don't hurry we'll miss your uncle's funeral, and you are not getting married 'til after your second Pulitzer and your own cooking show. Now, let's go…
>   (*Exits*)
>
>   (*Emma waves weakly at Alex. Neither speaks as Alex backs off stage.*)

ALEX:
Sweet dreams, Emma!
>   (*Exits*)

EMMA:
>   (*Turns to Sarah, aside*)

In constant motion or constant detour around the fallen pieces of her life which she tries to flatten on the road to my success.

Briefly: I come from a family that is used to prodigies, natural wonders, and generations of women that make tough acts to follow. I strive to continue that line of powerful women. I persevere in spite of….

SARAH:
Emma!

EMMA:
In spite of…

SARAH:
Let's go, kiddo.

EMMA:
But then…everything is in spite of something, isn't it. In my immediate family, when one of us fails, we are all punished by the mistaken party's refusal to eliminate themselves from the world of the perfect. Mom will tell you this is an adventure—this is what she's always wanted. But this romantic surge is really just a side effect of defeat.

BEA:

(*Entering*)
Is that my girls? Yes! My girls are here!

EMMA:

(*to us*)
That's my grandmother, who calls me "Bug" with the kind of accent responsible for Eudora Welty's entire career. Her name is Beatrice and she is, among other things, very sick. Her impenetrable battle-mode keeps her healthy, even though the enemy is her health. A heart-something, I think…broken after Granpa died last summer and now uncle Ben…. But she's tough, so a year of bereavement just looks like high blood pressure.

BEA:

Oh thank heaven my girls are finally here!

SARAH:

(*Entering*)
Road work near Richmond…but we made it. How are you?

BEA:

Fine, Fine. Everything is fine. Your brother's service was so nice.

SARAH:

We missed it?

BEA:

It was small. How are you?

SARAH:

Fine. We missed it?

BEA:

Good…Where's my Bug? Is that her?! Yes! I was getting worried I might have to walk to wherever your mother's taking us…

EMMA:

Florida.

BEA:

In a Winnebago! How liberating.

(Emma smiles and runs to Bea who spreads her arms like a quilt to cover them both. They stay inside each other's hug for an uncomfortable amount of time according to Sarah who watches, fidgeting.)

SARAH:

Okay…ready to go?

(They still hug)

(Sarah speaks to us)

SARAH:

For every stupid action there is an equal and stupid reaction. This is mine. Mark left with his girl, and I left with…ours.
(Changing her tone)
See, this is actually perfect, what I've always wanted. What is essential in all humans, born or broken. To just go. Inspiration like Whitman and the great ramblers, at our fingertips. Adventure, poetic release, freedom!!
Then there's my mother who's always lived a miniature life and is not going to be living any kind of life soon so I'm giving her this gift too—this gift of glorious wandering. And Ben…It's the least I could do,

EMMA:

Lord knows you want to do the least.

SARAH:

(to us)
I know this sounds crazy…

EMMA:
(Aside)
Pray for temporary insanity.

SARAH:
(Sighing)
Ah well.

EMMA:
(Unnoticed by Sarah)
Oh God.

SARAH:
It could be worse.

EMMA:
It will be.

SARAH:
Live and learn.

EMMA:
Die and regret.

SARAH:
The first day of the rest of our…

EMMA:
Oh god…

SARAH:
Carpe D…

EMMA:
(Finally Sarah hears her)
Don't.

(Sarah exits)

So here I am. Not really sure where I am. The South somewhere—south of home.

(Car engine revs as lights dim to black.)

- SCENE ONE -

(Sarah is driving, steering wheel in one hand, trivia book in the other humming/singing the words she knows on the radio. Emma is writing at the stationary covered table and curls can of corn as a hand weight. Bea is in the back looking out the window, contentedly hugging a colorfully decorated urn hidden under a black cloth.)

EMMA:
"Dear Sir, comma, this might be the silliest thing I've ever done in my life, comma, but it might just be an adventure, period."

SARAH:
(to herself)
"And miles to go before I sleep, comma, And miles to go before I sleep, period." Robert Frost.

EMMA:
I know.
(Writing again)
"My name is Emma. I know it's hard to trust someone based solely on his or her words, so I'll use someone else's…"The gentleness of all the gods go with thee!"—from *Twelfth Night*. I believe you were in the film version, correct?"

SARAH:
"Good-by my fancy! Farewell dear mate, dear love! I'm going away, I know not where…" *We're* going away, huh?

EMMA:
That poem is about death, mother.

SARAH:
What?

EMMA:
The speaker of that poem is going to die.

SARAH:
What?

EMMA:
It's Whitman it…Nevermind.

SARAH:
(Suddenly, reading from the book)
Hey, Kiddo! What is the capital of the Peoples Democratic Republic of Yemen?

EMMA:
(Not looking up)
Aden.

SARAH:
Yes! Beautiful! Answer the following about the People's Democratic Republic of Yemen.

EMMA:
Mom. I'm writing.

SARAH:
Monetary unit?

EMMA:

Yemeni Dinar.

SARAH:

Language?

EMMA:

Arabic.

SARAH:

Bordering body of water?

EMMA:

Red Sea. Are we done?

SARAH:

Colors on the flag including white?

EMMA:

Red, black, blue and white. Can we stop now?

SARAH:

Yeah sure. Just trying to have a little fun, intravenously. You are so damn good at knowing stuff. I love it!

EMMA:

They're facts, Mom. In a book. With words. That anyone can read.

SARAH:

And many do I'm sure, but why should I when I have you? What are you doing?

EMMA:

Uh, writing a letter to…

SARAH:

No, with that can? Like a hand weight! Oh, how smart! Hand me one.
    (Curling the can)
Just lift 'em like this?

EMMA:

Uh…yeah.

SARAH:

Wow…you are so brilliant! A workout and a side dish.
    (Quickly shifting her attention to the road, dropping the can on the ground)
Oh my god. Oh my *god*! Look! Did you see that guy? That's hilarious. Did you see that?!

EMMA:

No. What?

SARAH:

That guy's bumper sticker. "If you're not a hemorrhoid, get off my ass." "Get off my *ass*!" That's hilarious!

EMMA:

I think it's disgusting.

SARAH:

I thought it was funny.
Capital of Madagascar?

EMMA:

Working, Mother…

SARAH:
Why are you "working, Mother" all the time? This is a vacation, this is fun!

EMMA:
No comment.

SARAH:
Stop "working, Mother" and check on your grandma…We've passed at three fried pie stands and I haven't heard a peep.

EMMA:
Bea?

BEA:
Yes, Bug?

EMMA:
You still breathing?

BEA:
Very deeply, thank you.

EMMA:
She's fine.
    (Goes back to writing)

SARAH:
You hungry? Scribbling can be pretty strenuous.

EMMA:
If you're actually asking—I'd like real food. Not cereal, since that's all you thought to bring.

SARAH:

Then no, I wasn't *actually* asking. You want "real" food, you pick the nuts out of the Müslie.

EMMA:

Should I shoot myself now or wait for a gas station?

SARAH:

Not funny.

EMMA:

I'm serious mother, this is beyond stupid I…

>   *(Stops herself from erupting. Pause as she breathes. The directly to Sarah,)*

Can we *please* stop, now? I think I'm getting *scurvy*.

SARAH:

Looks like we've got…an eat-all-you-can or bare-all-you-can…better stay inside. Walk around the cabin Kiddo, that's why we got her. Wide aisles, lots of space.

EMMA:

Oh. I thought you were planning to get old and *fat* in here.

SARAH:

What a well-developed sense of humor.

EMMA:

We *are* running away aren't we? So we can all deteriorate together without regard to the rest of the world.

SARAH:

"Two roads diverged in a wood, and I, I took the one less traveled by…"

EMMA:
Less traveled by?

SARAH:
Absolutely.

EMMA:
The interstate?

SARAH:
We're not *running* from anything, my dear. It's much more of a flight, a soar! And *that* will make all the difference.

EMMA:
Je n'veut pas voler.

SARAH:
I don't speak French, darling. Get me a drink.

EMMA:
The word "to fly" in French means the same as "to steal." How ironic.
   (goes back to writing.)
"It is a beautiful thing to see someone my age perform so honestly on screen."
   (to herself)
Underline "my age."

SARAH:
Who's your age?

EMMA:
No one.

SARAH:
Who's your age? Who are you writing to?

EMMA:
No one, Mother.

SARAH:
He "*performs honestly*" does he?

EMMA:
Would you just drive, please?

SARAH:
He's an *actor* I hope.

EMMA:
Leave me alone.

SARAH:
Writing to an actor in Hollywood? What is it like to be you? Believing in such human dignity.

EMMA:
You don't have to believe in much to believe in the postal service.

SARAH:
People hardly use ink anymore—it's a statement of faith to send off a letter, especially to…does this actor know you?

EMMA:
No. That's why I'm writing.

SARAH:
Oh! It's so precious your blessed naivete.

EMMA:
Just. Drive.

SARAH:

What are you going to do with a Hollywood pen pal? Or what are they going to do with you?

EMMA:

I don't know, be friends, have mutual respect. If that's still legal.

SARAH:

Optimism has gotten way out of hand in this country.
Try to mail *that*. Only a poet could come close to capturing mountains on paper.

EMMA:

I'm not a poet.

SARAH:

"Beauty is truth, truth beauty,—that is all / Ye know on earth, and all Ye need to know."

EMMA:

Are we going to stop? Cause I'm fermenting here.

SARAH:

Poetry is our way out and back *in* to ourselves, not movies. Movies you sit through, poetry you live through. I mean just look outside, Emma. Tangible verse!
Why don't you just look?

EMMA:

Why?!! Because if I did look up for too long I would remember that my mother has kidnapped me and the elderly heart patient, that happens to be my grandmother, in a Winnebago heading to the edge of the continent, with no fruit or real food only Little Debbie Snack Cakes and Cheerios. So it's Hollywood or reality. And *Hollywood* makes *a lot* more sense.

(silence)

SARAH:

You don't like Little Debbies?

EMMA:

Anything you packed with a shelf life of over 20 years makes this vagary a little too permanent.

SARAH:

Permanent?

EMMA:

Yes, Mother. Permanent. Like death.

SARAH:

Well there is just no talking to you…and who would want to anyway! You're all death and Movie stars. I'm so thirsty all of a sudden…

EMMA:

Movie stars and Death. Neither of which you know anything about.

SARAH:

What the hell is that supposed to mean? Gimme a coke.

EMMA:

I am beyond expecting things from adults so I don't expect *you* to understand this at all. You can't possibly imagine what it's like to be in movies, to do something so amazing…to live so many times and all so perfectly…to be vulnerable, and powerful, and subtle, and valiant, and…
 (Fingering the letters.)
Watching those movies, him in those movies…it's this anxious ache like a huge, silver knife at your belly—not cutting you, but close enough to make you nervous, to make you condense and pay attention. Not pain, but hunger…and his knife sways so you can't ever relax and I don't want to cause he might leave…and I want to cry and I can't breathe, and I gleam…because there's so much more…

That is movies.

SARAH:

That's an orgasm.

EMMA:

Mom....

SARAH:

Trust me.

EMMA:

Usually when one's brother dies you try to make it to the funeral. *That* is death.

SARAH:

Jesus. You know I tried. It's not my fault this stupid boat broke. I can't change a tire. Jesus.

EMMA:

Remorse is also customary I've heard.

SARAH:

I do feel bad, Emma. Don't think I don't. I hadn't seen Ben in years and just as I was finishing a nice letter to him, he up and dies. I feel terrible. Y'know?

EMMA:

No, I don't. He's not my brother.

SARAH:

He's your family. Open this for me…

EMMA:

I don't know anything about him, Mom. I know he died and we missed the funeral. That's it.

SARAH:

We sent him a Christmas card every year.

EMMA:

That was nice of us.

SARAH:

Don't be pissy, I already feel bad enough.

EMMA:

You should. You never saw you brother even at his own funeral.

SARAH:

Good God, kid. I *did* see him. After your father and I married we just never made it down that far…very often.

EMMA:

To Carolina? You couldn't make it to Carolina? You live two states north?

SARAH:

He was always moving around, going places. Then you were born…

EMMA:

Don't blame your mistake on me.

SARAH:

It wasn't a mistake. We each had our own lives.

EMMA:

I had my own damn life! *DAMMIT!*

(Quite suddenly hits her pillow repeatedly.)
(Stops. Returns to her letter. Silence.)

SARAH:
(After a moment)
PMS?

EMMA:
Cabin Fever.

SARAH:
Already?

EMMA:
I'm sorry.

SARAH:
Me too.

EMMA:
I'm trying…

SARAH:
Okay.

EMMA:
Trying.

SARAH:
Okay.
(Silence. Then gingerly,)
Do you want to….

                              EMMA:
Turn around? Yes.

                              SARAH:
Talk about it?

                              EMMA:
Never worked before.

                              SARAH:
Kiddo I'm...
I can't believe you don't remember him.

                              EMMA:
Who?

                              SARAH:
Ben. Your Uncle.

                              EMMA:
I don't.

                              SARAH:
That's too bad.

                              EMMA:
Yeah.

                              SARAH:
He was smart like you. He was a painter. in love, all the time.

                              EMMA:
Any kids? Wife?

SARAH:

Neither. He was gay.

EMMA:

Really?

SARAH:

No not *really* gay...Not flaming. But it was obvious to Mom as soon as he got to high school. Then he left home, followed some guy, completely changed.... I don't know. I guess he thought I was disapproving or something...

EMMA:

(sarcastically)

Really.

SARAH:

...but I wasn't. I just didn't get it. *So*, I would *watch* instead of participating in his life. You know, like trying to figure out the rules to a football game from the stands. It looks so complicated...so easy to get hurt. Why would you ever do something so dangerous when you could just walk away...come home.
But he made it and he was happy his entire life. I just missed most of it. Now he's dead. So I feel bad.

(Pause)

EMMA:

Bea?

BEA:

Yeah, Bug?

EMMA:

Mom feels bad about Uncle Ben.

BEA:

Tell your Mom to stop worrying…she's fine; I'm fine; Ben's fine. He's got a great view of the mountains.

EMMA:

(Repeating to Sarah)
You're fine, she's fine, and Ben has a great view of something.

SARAH:

What was that?

EMMA:

Ben has something…back there.

SARAH:

Ben who?

EMMA:

(Repeating to Bea)
Ben who?

BEA:

Your brother Ben. Uncle Ben. *Dead* Ben.

SARAH:

What the hell is she talking about?

EMMA:

What the hell are you talking…

SARAH:

Don't curse in front of your grandma.

BEA:

What the hell are ya'll talking about up there?

SARAH:

What are *you* talking about Ma? Ben is what?

BEA:

Right here. He always said he'd never be caught *dead* in one of these road boats…

SARAH:

Now I'm confused. Ben is here? He's here? In the car?

BEA:

In the back. In the pot.

SARAH:

Why?! Why is Ben here…there…in a pot?!

BEA:

Well, I can't just leave him on the TV, can I?

EMMA:

Neat! Can I see him?
(Goes to get the urn)

BEA:

Sure. Take him up front. He needs some variety.

SARAH:

You brought him?

BEA:

I thought that was the point. To bring him so we could dump him when we got to the ocean.

SARAH:

Dump my brother?

EMMA:

Here he is!

> *(Emma uncovers the brightly painted urn adorned with stucco collage and feathers)*

BEA:

Scatter I mean. Scatter in the ocean, like he wanted…Oh! You missed that part didn't you? I keep thinking you were at the funeral.

EMMA:

> *(to the urn)*

I've never really met you before.

SARAH:

> *(to Emma)*

Yes you did Emma.
> *(to Bea)*

No I wasn't Mom.

EMMA:

> *(to Sarah)*

Well it's not real if I can't remember it.
> *(to the urn)*

You're dashing.

BEA:

Thank you, Bug. I made it myself. Ben got into stucco and taught me a few things. I may have got a bit overboard on the feathers but…

EMMA:

No I like it. Very…triumphant. What was he like Bea?

BEA:
Ben? Ohhhh…funny as hell. Very handsome, very kind. A good boy. Oh…which reminds me…I have some of his things I thought you two might want. You missed the distribution of Ben's things…the lovely oak armoire he had. That's for me.
    (Retrieves the gifts)
But I did snag these little treasures for ya'll.

SARAH:
I swear I'm going to crash.

BEA:
This is for you, Emma.
    (Hands her a book)

EMMA:
"Collected Works of Six American Poets". Oh thanks, Bea!

BEA:
It was Ben's…I thought you'd appreciate it.

SARAH:
It was mine, I gave it to him.

EMMA:
It's wonderful. The pages are so old.

SARAH:
Not *that* old.

BEA:
    (Pulling out another object)
And…this is for Sarah…when you get a chance. It's his camera. The one he used to shoot your wedding. Remember?

(Clicks a picture of Sarah)

SARAH:
Yes. Thanks.

EMMA:
Mom, isn't this great! A new friend.

SARAH:
Excellent.

EMMA:
He was gay?

BEA:
Very much so—both definitions.

EMMA:
What did Grandpa think about it?

BEA:
He didn't really understand, but I don't think he cared much. What do you think?

EMMA:
He liked Whitman. He's good in my book.

SARAH:
It's *my* book.

BEA:
And he was a writer like you. Wrote in his journal every night…poems and such.

EMMA:

Well, I'm not a poet…

BEA:

Never let anyone see any of it though. Not till last night did I ever see what he wrote. About me, about him, your sister, his…friends.

SARAH:

Emma's like that too! Always writing…never lets anyone into that head though. A secret since first grade!

EMMA:

(Shutting her out)
I don't have many friends but I have a journal.

BEA:

You have a journal?

EMMA:

I do. Well, kind of, it's just for dreams. I remember what I saw during the night and I write it down as soon as I get up, sometimes before. Sometimes I wake up and there's already a few words on the page and I don't even remember how they got there…
(Playing with the urn)

SARAH:

(to Emma)
Be careful honey…

EMMA:

I used to have awful dreams. Monsters and ghosts and everything. So Mom said I should try and write them all down in a book and see how scary they were on paper. When I started thinking about it…they really weren't that bad. Kinda funny actually.

BEA:
That's the healthiest thing a person can do is write to themselves.

EMMA:
I started when I was 6.

BEA:
Well your gonna live forever!

EMMA:
I write to movie stars too.

BEA:
It was so hard for him, people weren't as open as it is now. Ben wrote so…honestly about his life. Being gay…when he found out. *How* he found out if you know what I mean…

EMMA:
Oh yeah.

SARAH:
Oh god.

BEA:
And I never ever got to read it 'til now. And he's gone. Not *gone*…but I can't talk to him. I wish I could…Tell him how good he was, how proud we were…

EMMA:
Wow…
    (Passing the urn between her hands absently)

SARAH:
Can I…
    (Grabs the urn forcibly from Emma, sets it down in the seat)
Thanks.

BEA:

(Suddenly)
Would you mind if I read yours—your journal? I know that's usually a family no-no, but…I just wish I could've talked to Ben about his…he was a mystery to me 'til yesterday…and I'd love to read yours while you're right here next to me.
(Realizing it was a bad idea)
I…I'm sorry, Bug. I know that's stupid. Never mind.

EMMA:

No. No. I mean, Yes you can. If you'd really like to.

BEA:

Really?

SARAH:

Really?

EMMA:

Yeah. As long as you don't tell Mom my secrets.

BEA:

Promise.
(to Sarah)
Promise you won't ask me, Sarah?
(to Emma)
She knows I'm a sucker for gossip.

(Emma and Bea both look at Sarah.)

SARAH:

Yeah. Promise.

BEA:
Oh this is great. This makes me so very happy, Bug. Oh I can't wait. I can't wait! I know you'll be in my top 3 favorite writers of the universe!

EMMA:
Who're the others?

BEA:
Ben.
And John Grisham…Don't tell Ben though.

EMMA:
No problem.
    (They laugh)

BEA:
So. Where do we start? You've been writing since you were six?

EMMA:
They're a little dry at first but…It starts getting good around 4th grade, hold on a sec.
    (Emma goes to retrieve journal.)

    (Pause)

SARAH:
This is all very surprising.

BEA:
What?

SARAH:
Emma, handing over her journal like that. You're lucky.

BEA:

She's made me very happy, Sarah. I might just make it.

SARAH:

She doesn't write as much as she used to. She writes to movie stars now.

BEA:

She mentioned that. I though it was a joke. I think that's wonderful!

SARAH:

Wonderful?

BEA:

(to Emma)
Like who?

SARAH:

Who what?

BEA:

What film stars have you talked to, Bug?

EMMA:

A whole bunch. I started about two months ago. Now I've gotten pretty much everyone who's won anything in the last four years.
(Handing the journal to Bea)
Here's the most recent one. It's not done yet.

SARAH:

There're more? Where are they?

EMMA:

Home.

BEA:
Not finished yet? Well we'll just have to find some adventure to fill it with. Did you keep a journal, Sarah? I can't remember…Unless you hid it so well I…

SARAH:
No. I didn't.

BEA:
That's a shame.

SARAH:
I guess.

BEA:
I would've loved to read the early writings of the Pope.

EMMA:
The who?

BEA:
The Pope, Emma. Didn't you know your mother wanted to be the Pope when she was little?

EMMA:
You're joking…

SARAH:
Dead serious.
    (to the urn)
Sorry.

EMMA:
You wanted to be the Pope? You actually told someone that?

SARAH:

I know.

EMMA:

Mom, there are no female Popes. It's like a rule.

SARAH:

(Dramatically)
Can heaven be so envious!

BEA:

We weren't even Catholic.

SARAH:

We weren't even moral.

EMMA:

At least my flight of fancy is a hobby. Yours was an entire religion! That's hilarious. Were you serious?

SARAH:

Serious as a train wreck.

BEA:

I could've spawned a pope.

EMMA:

That sounds like heresy.

BEA:

Sounds like a hard act to follow.

EMMA:

There wouldn't be much of an act to follow, really. Celibacy is a pretty big deal over there, right?

SARAH:

(Dramatically)
Correct again, my beautiful, rational Emma. The world would've missed all your glory and be stuck with mine.

EMMA:

Well…
(The laughter dies)

BEA:

(Sinking into herself. Bea is having heart trouble)
Oh…

SARAH:

But there would only be one man in my life, and he would want nothing from me but devotion and prayer. The only other women near him would be celibate nuns. I think I could've handled that.

BEA:

Jesus…

SARAH:

Exactly. Me and Jesus…no marriage to worry about, no changing of minds in the middle of someone else's life. No cooking or cleaning, either! I mean he's already had his Last Supper.
(Chuckles)

EMMA:

Bea?

BEA:

Ohhh…

SARAH:

A foot-wash a day keeps the doctor away…

EMMA:

Mom!

SARAH:

What? Oh god. Mom?

BEA:

Yes. I'm fine…I just can't…

SARAH:

Momma, what? What?

BEA:

It's just a little hiccup…heart burn…. Ahhhhh…

SARAH:

Emma, get the wheel.

EMMA:

What?

SARAH:

Drive, Emma!

(Emma runs to the driver's seat)

BEA:

Sarah, don't make her do that.

EMMA:
(Panicked)
How do I do it?

SARAH:
Gas, Brake, Go. Stay on the road, avoid trees and slow children.

EMMA:
(Gripping the wheel)
Mom!

SARAH:
What?

EMMA:
(Reviewing)
Gas, break…

SARAH:
Go!

EMMA:
Okay!

(They switch places. Emma driving, Sarah runs to Bea)

SARAH:
Mom, when did this start? Just now?

BEA:
Five minutes ago. I don't know. Sarah…

SARAH:

I can handle this, Mom. Don't worry.

BEA:

Well someone has to! "Gas, Brake, Go?!" Get that child back here.
    (calling)
Emma!

EMMA:

Yes!

BEA:

Get back here.

    (Emma swerves, recovers.)

SARAH:
    (Grabbing the wheel)
No No No!
    (to Emma)
You stay.

BEA:
    (Squeezing herself)
Oh god…

SARAH:
    (Running in between Bea and Emma)
Mom, breathe. Emma, hold on.

EMMA:

That's really the only thing I know how to do…

BEA:

You're doing great!

SARAH:

(to Bea)
You. Don't talk anymore…

BEA:

I just need to rest. It gets better when I rest…

SARAH:

(To Emma).
The doctors already told me about this. She's fine, we're fine.

EMMA:

I'm fine.

SARAH:

Yes. You are very, very fine.

EMMA:

Mom?

SARAH:

Yes?

EMMA:

That sign said to "watch for falling rocks". Should I be nervous?

SARAH:

No.

EMMA:

Then I'm fine.

SARAH:

Ok. Keep driving.

BEA:

Emma!

SARAH:

Mom, don't scream, you'll break yourself.

EMMA:

Yes?

BEA:

What do you say to your movie stars?

SARAH:

Not now, Mom.
(Getting a first aid box and bags of pills)

BEA:

(to Sarah, whispering)
I don't want her to see me like this. Get her to read me some letters.

SARAH:

She can't, Mom. She's driving.

BEA:

(to Emma)
You can remember something.

EMMA:

Should I go to a hospital?

BEA:
(almost hysterically)
Impress me, Bug! Pretend I'm Jimmy Stewart!

SARAH:
No. She's fine. Just say something...

EMMA:
(Scared now)
Mom?

SARAH:
YES.

EMMA:
Jimmy Stewart's dead.

BEA:
EMMA!

SARAH:
Just say something

EMMA:
I think we should go to a doctor.

SARAH:
Something else.

(Alex appears and, unseen to Bea and Sarah.)

EMMA:
Okay!
(Stumbling)

"Dear…" I don't know…

(Alex takes over the wheel for Emma, relieved, who watches the scene in back.)

BEA:

Oh…Jesus…right there, it hurts right there…I'm deflating.

SARAH:

How long since you saw Dr. Regal?

BEA:

Two weeks. I hate doctors. Gimme the nitroglycerin. Emma's not listening?

SARAH:

(Gets it from the bag)
No. Would you concentrate, Mom. What else did the doctor give you?

BEA:

He said take some new drug to thin my blood.

SARAH:

Coumadin.

BEA:

Yes. But I still get dizzy and nose bleeds and…

SARAH:

Breathe Mom.

BEA:

…not stop for hours…

SARAH:

The nose bleeds?

BEA:

Yes.

SARAH:

Hours?

BEA:

I don't know it starts real suddenly, but if I sit it calms down.

SARAH:

How long do you sit?

BEA:

I…I can't remember.

SARAH:

Why can't you, Mom?

BEA:

I just go to sleep.

SARAH:

Pass out or go to sleep?

(Alex replaces Emma's hands on the wheel and leaves.)

BEA:

I don't know, Sarah.

SARAH:

Just lie down.

EMMA:

Mom!

SARAH:

Yes Emma.

EMMA:

I forgot which one was the brake!

SARAH:

Oh God! Hold on Mom.
    (Runs to Emma)

BEA:

Holding dear.
    (Falls to sleep quickly)

EMMA:

Mom!

SARAH:

I'm here. I'm good. Let me…
    (Takes the wheel)
…and we are going to pull over
    (She does)
…And stop.
    (They do. Pause,)
Okay. Now you sit here and breathe.
    (Back to Bea)
Momma, we're stopped now so I can…Mom. Momma?

EMMA:

What's wrong?

SARAH:

Good. It's over.

EMMA:

Is she…is she…Mom is she…?

SARAH:

Oh, no, honey. No she's just sleeping.

(Emma looks shocked at Mom. Throws something violently.)

SARAH:

Emma? Emma, honey, what? What?

EMMA:

You said my fish was "just sleeping" before you flushed him down the toilet. You don't have to play those kid games with me anymore.

SARAH:

What….? Honey, honey, honey. No. It's not the same thing. She really is sleeping.

EMMA:

She's not fish sleeping?

SARAH:

No fish.

EMMA:

Okay.

(Goes to kiss Bea goodnight, takes Bea's hand and holds it looking at her face.)

She's still breathing.

SARAH:

See…that's good.

EMMA:

(Emma, shaken and slightly bruised by the experience retreats to her cot, passing Sarah without a kiss. Turns back.)

Are we sleeping here tonight?

SARAH:

Uh…yeah. Sure.

EMMA:

We're not moving anymore today?

SARAH:

No.
(Emma passes the urn and pats it goodnight. Goes to bed.)
Maybe I should pray. Dear Lord, Where the hell am I?
(Picks up camera and snaps a picture of herself)
One for the scrapbook.
(pause)
Why Why Why did you do this?
Leave me, leave Emma. Can you see what you've done to her? She mauls furniture and harasses celebrities. *That* is not my fault.
Well I can be stupid like all the bastards in the world. Because at least I have something of myself, just mine, that I have already donated to the fraternity of society. I've already done my job…and she is the most excellent, glorious girl in the world…!
(Throws something.)

EMMA:

G'night mom…

SARAH:

Hmm? Oh, g'night. Thanks for taking the wheel. And sorry I yelled at you. And sorry generally…for general things…

EMMA:

No problem…. I'm…

SARAH:

I know.

EMMA:

Goodnight.

    (Lights fade…but just to half. We hear the engine turn off and nightly cricket sounds. They are stopped for the night. Emma is asleep on her cot, and Mom is shutting the car down for the night.)

SARAH:

    (Sees the urn, picks it up)
Jesus, Ben you look like a hood ornament.
    (breath)
Mom said it was a good service. Sorry I missed it. I had a flat tire and a 16-year-old.

    (Puts him down overly-gently in front of her as though she would read to him. Opens the book of poetry and randomly flips to a page.)

Good choice.
    (reads from the book)

    (Alex appears from stage left. Walking boyishly into the cab he is invisible to Sarah. Walks directly to Emma and sits on her cot. Sarah's dialog is read over the following scene.)

SARAH:

<u>Advice</u>, by Langston Hughes. "Folks, I'm telling you, / birthing is hard/ and dying is mean—so get yourself / a little loving / in between."
    (Laughs)

    (Emma wakes slowly noticing Alex. She hugs him. Alex kisses Emma simply. Emma is overcome with sleep and nearly faints as Alex tucks the covers around her.)

ALEX:

G'night, Emma. Sweet Dreams…

EMMA:

Thank you.

(Alex leaves as quiet and overlooked as before.)

SARAH:

"A little loving in between…" At least I've got the "in between."

(Lights down)

- SCENE TWO -

(Lights up. The next morning. Bea is reading Emma's diary with lots of interest. Sarah and Emma look outside at the gas station.)

EMMA:

It says "open".

SARAH:

It's completely dark.

BEA:

Get some gum kay, Sarah?

SARAH:

I don't like this one.

EMMA:

(Rushing her)
Go, Mom. They're all the same.

SARAH:

Maybe we could…

EMMA:

Just GO!

SARAH:

Alright!

EMMA:

Wait!

(Runs to the table and ceremoniously licks, seals, and kisess four letters. Hands them to Sarah)

Now Go.

SARAH:

Yes Ma'am.

EMMA:

Handle with care.

BEA:

Get Carefree gum, Carefree.

SARAH:

I wish.

EMMA:

GO, Mother.

SARAH:

Okay, okay…be back in a sec

EMMA:
(Watching her like a home run)
And…she's…. gone.
(Retrieves a small black cell phone).

(Bea continues reading)

EMMA:
(Dials. Hangs up.)
Didn't answer.

(Bea laughs at her journal)

EMMA:
Is it always this hot here?

BEA:
Where are we now?

EMMA:
The Quickie Stop outside Chester, South Carolina.

BEA:
Yup. Air conditioning's the closest we have to winter. The only thing that changes is the wind. Sometimes it brings rain, sometimes bugs.

EMMA:
You know so much.

BEA:
Just about my home. Above the gnat-line and I'm helpless.
(Lifts Emma's journal)
But *this* stuff is fascinating.

EMMA:

It's a mess but…it's me, I guess.

BEA:

I've had this one. About the slide in the waterfall…

EMMA:

Oh yeah. I've had that one a couple times. I slide and slide but I never hit the water. I never get off.

BEA:

Me neither! It bugs me like bees.

EMMA:

Me too.

BEA:

The funny thing is I know when I'm going to have this dream. It's almost like I can feel the water or hear it or something. And I think "Stop it Bea, you can't get off"

(The phone rings. Emma lunges)

EMMA:

Dad? Hey, it's Emma. I'm okay…I was wondering…what good news? I what? A letter? For me! Oh God, really! Does it say who sent—? Oh my GOD! What? When?…Why aren't you staying with me?…WAIT, Uh…We're coming home right now. Mom just said so. Yeah! We're turning around and coming home right now. Mom just said this whole trip was a stupid, stupid idea and we're turning around as we speak. Wait for me. Dad…

SARAH:

I love the smell of Frito's in the morning.

(Re-entering)
Ready or not…here we go!

(*Noticing Emma*)
Hey where'd you get a Walkman?

EMMA:

(*Hiding the phone*)
A what? Yeah. It's a...whatever.
Dad...listen...you can't just pick up and leave like that...

SARAH:

Did the Butler forget to make my coffee again?

BEA:

I think you forgot the butler.

EMMA:

(*Into the phone*)
No, I know Mom did but...I don't want to be here...We've got so much more together than apart.

BEA:

Gum?

SARAH:

Yeah. What is she doing?
(*Flips Bea the gum*)

EMMA:

(*Into the phone*)
Dad...I love you. Please don't...

SARAH:

Emma? What is that?

EMMA:

It's mine.

SARAH:

It's a cell phone.

EMMA:

(*Into the phone*)
Daddy, no....

SARAH:

Where'd you get a cell phone? Who are you talking to?
(*Takes phone*)
Hello?...Mark...I...
(*Hangs up phone.*)

EMMA:

Mom!
(*Grabs the phone and tries to re-dial*)

SARAH:

Did he give you this? Your father?

EMMA:

No he gave me two hundred dollars. I bought it. It's mine.

SARAH:

What? Why would he do that?

EMMA:

My birthday...mom I need to talk with him it's important!

SARAH:

Your birthday isn't for three weeks.

EMMA:

He didn't know when he'd see me again. He didn't know when he would be leaving us.

SARAH:

But you knew?
So this is a conspiracy.

EMMA:

I've got two letters in the mail today. Mom this is so big! We have to turn around.

SARAH:

Two letters from whom?

EMMA:

Actors, Mom! We have to go back, now!

SARAH:

We're not moving.

EMMA:

…moving to Seattle.

SARAH:

What?

EMMA:

Dad is moving to Seattle. I have important mail. We have to go back. That's what I was trying to tell him before you hung up.

SARAH:

He's…?

EMMA:

Moving to Seattle. Saturday. With that woman.

(*Pause*)

SARAH:

I don't care.

EMMA:

I do. Mom, we have to turn around!

SARAH:

This is great.

EMMA:

No, this is real. Take me back. I want to go back.

SARAH:

No you don't you just want your postcards.

EMMA:

I want Dad.

SARAH:

We don't need him.

EMMA:

I want home.

SARAH:

We don't need it!

BEA:

You need to listen to your daughter.

SARAH:
You think this is my fault that he's bribing her—That's my fault? For God's sake!

BEA:
For her sake. It's not your fault but she is your daughter. Talk to her.

(Pause)

SARAH:
(Points to the phone)
Digital?

EMMA:
Yeah.

SARAH:
Three way calling?

EMMA:
Yeah.

SARAH:
Voice messaging?

EMMA:
Yeah.

SARAH:
Consistent interstate service across the entire US?

EMMA:
Yes.

SARAH:

(*Pause*)
Want another one?

BEA:

That's not helping.

SARAH:

I tried. I can't compete. I give up.

EMMA:

Just take me home. We're only two days away, one day if we drive all night. Florida's not going anywhere.

SARAH:

Neither are we if we don't get moving.

EMMA:

Are we going back? Mom I have to get back.

SARAH:

Yeehaw.

EMMA:

Mom please…Dad's leaving us…and my letters…. I've got to be there…

SARAH:

If he's moving there won't be any there there.

EMMA:

He's keeping the house in Maryland too. He's saving it for us.

SARAH:

Well. A plague on both his houses.

(Car peels away)

- SCENE THREE -

(The Winnebago has stopped for the evening. The women are sitting outside in casual silence. Bea is reading Emma's journal, Emma writing another letter, Ben's urn is in between them. Sarah watches both like an outsider.)

EMMA:
(writing)
"If you ever have the time or mind to write, I'm intrigued with your performances. And I'm an excellent pen pal. Sincerely, Emma Macy."
(Pause. to Sarah)
We stopping here for good?

SARAH:
For tonight.

EMMA:
Good enough.
(Finishing her letter abruptly and completely she performs her ritual lick-seal-kiss on the letter.)
I'm going to bed.

SARAH:
Now?

EMMA:
It's dark now.

SARAH:
Okay…Don't let the bedbugs bite!

EMMA:
They never do.

SARAH:

G'night.

BEA:

Good night, Bug.

EMMA:

G'night, Grandma.
 (Pats Ben's urn Goodnight, heads to bed)

SARAH:

Hey Kid. Um…before you settle down…I just want to say, I'm sorry.

EMMA:

Look…

SARAH:

No. I want to say this now. I'm very sorry for this morning. For anything that makes us more separate than we should be.

EMMA:

Mom…

SARAH:

And I know mine and your father's situation must seem a little immature right now, but it's just change. Love makes one do strange things, and your father's…misgivings make him…But I still love him…I do. And maybe, if you and I work together, we can rope him back…after he sees all our adventures. Seattle has nothing on us. Together. Hm?

EMMA:

Yeah.

SARAH:
I was always planning on going back. I just wanted to make him nervous.

EMMA:
Really?

SARAH:
Yeah. Having a husband is a hard habit to break.

EMMA:
So's having a father.

BEA:
So's having a heart attack.

SARAH:
Parents do dumb stuff for attention.
(Sarah reaches to Emma for a hug. Emma quickly hugs her and moves away.)

EMMA:
Goodnight Mom…
(Goes to bed.)

SARAH:
She still have that phone with her?

BEA:
I guess.

SARAH:
It makes me nervous.

BEA:

Huh.

(Goes back to reading.)

(Alex enters, walking unnoticed through Bea and Sarah, and sits on the bed. She lifts her head)

EMMA:

Hey!

ALEX:

(With flair)
Good evening, Emma.

EMMA:

Good evening.

(They kiss. Both get up silently and button each other's jackets.)

SARAH:

What are you thinking about?

BEA:

Hmmm?

SARAH:

What are you reading about?

BEA:

Oh. Your daughter at age
(She checks)
…14?

SARAH:

Great…how's she doing?

BEA:

Waltzing with giraffe and antelope on the Serengeti.

SARAH:

Dreams are funny things.

BEA:

Ben was the same way…

SARAH:

Kids are funny things.

BEA:
(Looks at her)
Sometimes you talk like you don't know the first thing about being a mother.

SARAH:

I guess I'm just not very good at it.

BEA:

Maybe you haven't been paying attention. It's not hard if you just feed them, don't get in their way, and get excited when they do.

SARAH:

Easy as pie.

BEA:

When in your life have you ever made a pie?

SARAH:

Easy as…Oreos.
(Pause)
I talked to her. About us.

BEA:

Just now?

SARAH:

I said I was sorry.

BEA:

Congratulations.

SARAH:

I said it didn't I. I put the effort forth.

BEA:

I suppose.

SARAH:

What does that mean?

BEA:

Three minutes of quality time is a start. So we're turning around tomorrow?

SARAH:

No…maybe…I don't know. I don't know what I want. What about Ben?

BEA:

Ben would want you to be happy.

(Walking out of the cab Alex and Emma pass Sarah and Bea. Alex is still invisible to Sarah, but Bea seems to see something.)

EMMA:

I'm going for a walk.

SARAH:

Now?

EMMA:

It's beautiful now.

SARAH:

Honey...

EMMA:

I'll be back soon, okay.

SARAH:

We'll be waiting.

EMMA:

Don't be.

SARAH:

We will.

EMMA:

Don't. Bye.

BEA:

Bye, Bug.

EMMA:

Bye, Bea.
    (Kisses her cheek)

BEA:

Bring back something to write about, Okay? We've got to fill this book of yours.

EMMA:

Yes ma'am. Thanks Mom.

SARAH:

Did I miss the part where I said "okay"?
Okay.
    (Pause. Emma and Alex exit.)
Well.

BEA:

Well.

    (Pause. Bea laughs at the anecdote. Making it obvious that Sarah is missing something)

SARAH:

Well. I'm going to bed. Long day tomorrow.

BEA:

Alright. Take your brother.

    (Hands her the urn. Sarah takes it uneasily.)

SARAH:

Gotta be alert. Gotta be…punctual.

BEA:

Punctual? Good Lord, Sarah. You're just as bad as your father. If you have something to tell me, do it. Don't be "punctual."

SARAH:

What does she know about her dad?

BEA:

Not much. A lot of guessing. Fantasy. What do you know about your husband?

SARAH:

Not much, apparently.

BEA:

Baby...

(Cradles Sarah in her arms, They rock together.)

SARAH:

Does she miss him?

BEA:

I don't know much about dreams but I'd say she does. Though it's more as one would miss a staple in a dissertation. Everything is still all there, just not as organized.

SARAH:

Is it beautiful? Her writing?

BEA:

She's found a power in words.

SARAH:

I want to see it.

BEA:

You're not invited.

SARAH:

It's not even really about her...I mean it's her dreams, it's not like I'm going to find out about her sex life....
Right?

BEA:

Good Lord.

SARAH:

I said I was sorry.

BEA:

For what, exactly?

SARAH:

For whatever I did. Marrying the wrong man. Being stupid. Trying to show her what living should be like…the beauty of things. This trip is her freedom and she's too busy hating me

BEA:

Nobody hates you.

SARAH:

I'm the good guy here. I'm trying…I swear.

BEA:

Then don't.

SARAH:

What?

BEA:

Try. It's obviously not working. I don't think anything's gonna change until where you're going becomes more important than what your leaving. She's with you either way but she needs to see that you're with her.

SARAH:

I know.

BEA:

I like this trip. Your father would've loved it, so would your brother. We've got traveling in the blood. Just find your course.

SARAH:

I want to fix this. I do.
    (Brief pause)
How are *you*, Momma?

BEA:

Me? I need to pray. Other than that I'm doing fine.

SARAH:

We're not talking "last rights" are we?

BEA:

No, no. Just some productive silence.

SARAH:

Do you want to go to a doctor? I just thought…

BEA:

I hate doctors.

SARAH:

I know. Can I do anything?

BEA:

Not unless you can get His attention better than I can.

SARAH:

Doubt it.
    (Pause)
Was Ben…I mean was he okay? I'm a terrible person. I just…

BEA:

He was fine. Brave and ready. A little disappointed in longevity but tough.

SARAH:

I should've been down there more. I wanted to…

BEA:

Maybe. But he understood how people work. It was just different worlds.

SARAH:

Wait for her.

BEA:

Will do.
    (to Sarah and Ben's urn)
Good night, kids.

SARAH:

Goodnight.

(Sarah goes to bed.)

(Bea breathes deeply and looks at the sky.)

BEA:

Lord…What is this? An old woman looks up and remarks at the vastness of black before her. No city lights, no smog. Just the stars and left-over galaxies she read about in her husband's old *Discover* magazines. She peruses them like pages in her own story, asking the crystal crumbs why she sees their years of light and not her husband's.
Is he farther than light? Is he with you?
Shhh, Bea. You're talking to yourself again and that only leads people to distrust you. Lord knows that's all I've got now—Trust and pills.

(Alex re-enters carrying Emma. She is asleep in his arms and comfortably rolls into a curl as he deposits her on her cot. As he tucks her in.)

ALEX:

Sweet dreams, Emma.

EMMA:
(Without consciousness)
Thank you.

(Alex slowly and quietly straightens his clothes and walks out the front door passing Bea as he exits.)

BEA:
Hi, there.

ALEX:
(Startled)
Hello.

(Silence)

BEA:
Hi there.

ALEX:
Hi.

BEA:
That was kind the way you carried her back, tucked her in. Do you always do that for her? Every night?

ALEX:
Yes ma'am.

BEA:
Every night? She's mighty lucky.

ALEX:
I suppose we both are.

BEA:
You're Irish too. My husband's family was Irish.

ALEX:
Coincidence.

BEA:
I doubt it. I'm surprised she didn't mention that.

ALEX:
I suppose I don't talk that much.

BEA:
Really?

ALEX:
Yes Ma'am. I let her. She falls asleep if I do.

BEA:
Well I'll keep that in mind in our discussion.

ALEX:
Uh ma'am…how is it that you can all of a sudden *see* me?

BEA:
(*Holds up Emma's journal.*)
I read about you.

ALEX:
Oh.

BEA:
She dreams you often…Calls you "moon eyes".

ALEX:

Really?

BEA:

(Looks at his eyes)
Yup. De-fin-ite-ly moony. Alex isn't it?

ALEX:

Yes.

BEA:

Pleasure. Beatrice Leary.

ALEX:

The Grandmother, right?

BEA:

Yes.

ALEX:

She talks a lot of you too.

BEA:

Really?

ALEX:

Quite. Thinks you know about everything there is.

BEA:

Oh I find things to be dumb about.

(Pause)

So what do you look for in a woman?

ALEX:

Pardon?

BEA:

You've been hanging around us long enough, I thought you might be looking for something in particular.

ALEX:

Not looking anymore. If you mean…

BEA:

I don't really know what I mean.
Are you an angel? Am I going to die tonight? You can tell me. I'm fine with it…At one time in my life I would've died for someone with your eyes anyway.

ALEX:

What?

BEA:

Your eyes. My husband had eyes like yours, so did my son—polished, baby blue. Am I going to die?

ALEX:

Eventually I suppose. But not because of me, I assure you. And not tonight, I hope.

BEA:

Hmm. Well that's all right. I would hate the angel of death to be dating my granddaughter anyway.

ALEX:

Me too. I don't think I could compete much.

BEA:

No, I don't think so either. Will you sit?

ALEX:

Thank you.

BEA:

You remind me of someone I met a long time ago in New York City. If you don't mind a story?

ALEX:

Not at all. A good night for listening.

BEA:

Good. I grew up in Georgia, with nothing doing but magazines and movies. But I went once to New York, all by myself, the day I graduated college. Went just to see a show, just one. But that's not the point...

ALEX:

Sure it is.

BEA:

There was a boy, looked just like you, who took my ticket at the window. He had your eyes; big. And your cheeks too; flushed like a peach. Perfect symmetry, making him easy to look at and hard to take seriously. Lips ruddy like paint. He wore a blue coat, black buttons like river pebbles, brown shoes, and...but that's not my point...

ALEX:

Sure it is.

BEA:

The show was starting. Lights dimming and dusky. Orchestra was charged and babbling with music. You came over and asked to sit.
I didn't say anything all through Act One. I was confused to be honest. I had not expected attention in this city. You left before intermission but came back as the lights went down again—dusk again.

You touched me...
> *(Touches his arm)*

right there, to explain which songs were your favorites. You loved every one. You held me here...
> *(Touches his hands)*

through the after-show crowd, past the theatre, above the streets, in between the lights, up to the tops,...you kissed me here
> *(Touches his cheek)*

before the evening rushed a new morning. But, you found me again the next day...and I married you the next month and...Oh, I loved you.

ALEX:

Bea...

BEA:

It's so hard not being with you. Not seeing you every day. And I know it's self I'm talking for...but you knew me longer than anyone else. You knew me. You knew me.

(Alex hugs Bea)

ALEX:

I do still. I don't know you any less.

BEA:

It's so hard not having that one thing that makes the most sense. *Entirety* is so hard without you. And *calm* is so hard...and *anticipation*.

ALEX:

Of?

BEA:

Dancing.

ALEX:

Anticipation of dancing?

BEA:

Would you?

ALEX:

I'd be honored.

BEA:

Really?

ALEX:

Of course.

(Bea stops and looks amazed at Alex. Afraid of what he is.)

(Getting in a slow dance position. The music starts. They dance, smiling. Bea begins to tire and gradually lets Alex lead her to her bed. He helps her into bed.)

ALEX:

Goodnight, Bea.

BEA:

Thank you

ALEX:

Sweet dreams.

(Alex is alone onstage. Facing the audience. Blackout)

- SCENE FOUR -

(Next morning. Emma is up writing at the table. Enter Bea, slightly groggy but awake.)

BEA:

Oh God.
(Her heart is starting again)
Oh God...

EMMA:

Bea? What? Are you sick?

BEA:

Bug. I...I need...

EMMA:

Are you okay? Should I call Mom? Do you need something?

BEA:

(Touches her heart and breathes)
No. I just got going too fast. I...

EMMA:

You're hurting again.

BEA:

I'm...ahhh.

EMMA:

I don't know what to do...
Mom!

BEA:

Don't wake her...Just...in her bag...

EMMA:

Are you sure...I can.

BEA:

The bag…Oh god…

EMMA:

The bag.
    (Goes to it.)

BEA:

The blue bottle…

EMMA:

    (Searching. To herself.)
Please, God, where are they…

BEA:

Ahh…

EMMA:

Please…
    (Finds them)
Here! I got them!

    (Runs back to Bea)

BEA:

Just a pill…

EMMA:

    (Gives her the pill)
Here.

BEA:

…makes it better.

EMMA:

Please…

BEA:

I'm…I'm good…
(Swallows pills and breathes.)

BEA:

I had a dream just now…it was Ben and I…and he was a prince and I must've been a princes or something royal cause I had a catch of blonde hair in spirals down to me heels. And everything looked so old. With stone castle walls and checker board fields…and Ben dressed like a knight…of course he had sky blue velvet cape over his armor.

EMMA:

Bea…?

BEA:

I'm fine…and Ben was just calling to me from below my window in the tower…

EMMA:

What did he say?

BEA:

Nothing. He was just calling, maybe singing…that's it, he was singing to me…Just music and…maybe I'll go back to bed and see if he takes requests.

EMMA:

That's a pretty dream.

BEA:

Yes.

EMMA:

Do you mind if I write it down?

BEA:

It'd be my honor and pleasure.
Why are you awake so early this morning?

EMMA:

We're going home today.

BEA:

Yes. Well…

EMMA:

Mom said we'd go back, today. We're going back today.

BEA:

Thank you for letting me read your journal, Bug.

EMMA:

You're welcome. I'm a little surprised I let you. My usual reaction to people reading my books is like me and beetles. I hate beetles.

BEA:

Me too.

EMMA:

And they're everywhere.

BEA:

I think they're good for both of us.

EMMA:

Beetles?

BEA:
Books…of dreams.

EMMA:
Right.

BEA:
We need them.
It's important to know about each other.

EMMA:
Are you teaching me something?

BEA:
I'm trying to figure you out.

EMMA:
Good luck.

BEA:
You got something to get through, something you don't believe in yet.

EMMA:
Mom says I believe in too much. Actors and airmail, specifically. What do you believe in?

BEA:
God and everything.

EMMA:
You believe in everything?

BEA:
I don't think I believe in nothing.

EMMA:

Will you stay with us?

BEA:

I'm not going anywhere your mom's not driving at this point.

EMMA:

Please stay with me.

BEA:

That sounds nice. You'd write to me though? If I didn't stay?

EMMA:

Yeah. But…

BEA:

Cause you write to movie stars.

EMMA:

That's different.

BEA:

Why? You write to them to…to get out? Is that what you said.

EMMA:

I'm breeding possibility.

BEA:

Possibility of what?

EMMA:

Of something wonderful, far away, that has nothing to do with me. Something I can expect but don't have to wait for.

BEA:

I see. You're writing your own fairy tale.

EMMA:

Making my life vicariously exciting. I mean, it's just a letter.

BEA:

To someone important.

EMMA:

I guess.

BEA:

You want to be a movie star?

EMMA:

I want to be anything. I want to be friends. I want to be out.

BEA:

I wouldn't know the first thing to say to a movie star.

EMMA:

I say, "You have great talent—you're an honest performer—and if you ever have the time or mind to write, I'm an excellent pen-pal. P.S. My doors are always open."

BEA:

An invitation.

EMMA:

I guess. But then they'd have to meet my parents.

BEA:
Well. I think that is a wonderful way to live. Really. I think you have purpose and initiative. You should run for president.

EMMA:
President of what?

BEA:
The United States of America. You've got enthusiasm and good grammar. I'd vote for you.

EMMA:
There's one.

BEA:
Maybe we're getting ahead of ourselves. Let's write to the president, first. Think of whom you could help if you had political sway.

EMMA:
I write to celebrities. My aspirations are purely selfish.

BEA:
No they're optimistic. You'd be a good famous person.

EMMA:
Then optimism is way out of hand in this country.
Oh my god. My mother said that.

BEA:
Optimism is the only way to change things. You start writing letters, then petitions, then bills, the State of the Union Addresses and YOU have successfully used a pen and paper to change the world. Good words move people…

EMMA:
Move people…

BEA:
...they bring people together, nations come back together...

EMMA:
Back together...

BEA:
...starts with one person's gumption. It's not selfish if you're not selfish.

EMMA:
(Agreeing)
Okay...

BEA:
Okay.

EMMA:
(Excited, getting ideas)
Okay!

BEA:
Can't hurt to try.

EMMA:
Can't hurt to try...Bea?

BEA:
Yes.

EMMA:
How do you make love?

(Pause)

BEA:

I have to tell you, that's about the only question I wasn't prepared to answer.

EMMA:

No, I mean make *people* love each other.... again.

BEA:

Well, Bug...Love is a tricky thing...Usually happens by accident.

EMMA:

Or design.

BEA:

If you're trying to make some *particular* love rekindle between a *certain* mother and father, I wouldn't push it...But I wouldn't doubt it either.

EMMA:

Okay.

BEA:

You can't force accidents.

EMMA:

Okay.

BEA:

Are you coming to bed? It's almost morning.

EMMA:

I have a lot of work to do. Enthuse the president, renovate my family...

BEA:

Sounds too tough for me. I leave the world in your hands, my dear.

BEA:	EMMA:
Sweet dreams…	Sweet dreams…

(They look at each other. Bea exits.)

- SCENE FIVE -

(An hour later, still early. Emma is up alone writing.)

EMMA:

Dear Mr. President, I am so glad to make your acquaintance, though I have never seen you in person only on C-Span. You are a marvelous leader and a fascinating man. My name is Emma. I would love to know what your favorite movie is. If you ever the time or mind to write, I'm intrigued and an excellent pen-pal. God Bless America, Emma Macy.

SARAH:

(Enters barely awake.)
Emma?

EMMA:

Mom! Good Morning. I moved to politicians!

SARAH:

What.

EMMA:

I thought, and Grandma did too, that since I'd had such good luck corresponding with movie stars, I should try to use my talents to affect some real change in the world. At least America, at first. So I'm writing politicians. National, State, even the UN or something.

SARAH:

Good morning.

EMMA:

Who's our Congressman?

SARAH:

Losing Hollywood so soon?

EMMA:

No. I'm just broadening my range of influence. Celebrities are one thing, I mean they definitely have a voice in people's lives, but the real decision makers are the politicians…and advertisers, but that's a mess I don't want to deal with 'til an election year.

SARAH:

Is this a career path I'm sensing? Writing letters?

EMMA:

Could be. Never been done before.

SARAH:

Living through the written word I approve of, but my daughter is not going to live through other people.

EMMA:

Yeah. Anyway, when are we going back? Cause, I'm running out of stamps and I need a better pen if I'm writing the White House.

SARAH:

Going back?

EMMA:

Home. Maryland. Dad.

SARAH:

Oh uhm…I don't know, Bug.

EMMA:

Mom...

SARAH:

I said I'd think about, and I just don't think it's a good idea to get in your father's way. If he wants Seattle, then...he can have it...I'm helpless.

EMMA:

No you're not.

SARAH:

Let's just get to Florida and then we'll decide.

EMMA:

No. We don't have time. You've got to try. I mean, talk about it. What if Dad knew just how you felt about him? I mean, he left without talking and we left without talking...one of you has to say something. And if you said the *right* something, if he heard the right something, then we could go home.
    (Changes her tone, encouraging, starting her plan)
You love him still.

(Emma secretively dials her father on the phone)

SARAH:

I do.

EMMA:

You want to go home.

SARAH:

I don't know. Yes...no...I want *him* home, *here* I mean. I want him here.

EMMA:

You want him here.

SARAH:

I mean I feel good out here. Spontaneous…carpe-ing as much diem as I can get. But all this is just wind without…

EMMA:

Dad.

SARAH:

Mark would love it here.

EMMA:

And you'd love him here.

SARAH:

And he doesn't…

EMMA:

Love that other girl.

SARAH:

I don't think so. Because…

EMMA:

He doesn't take her to museums.

SARAH:

Or surprise her. He just…

EMMA:

Had sex with her.

SARAH:

Yeah. And…

EMMA:

It's just little blunder in a confusing time. You can forgive a little blunder.

SARAH:

I hope. Oh god, I hope he comes back. I hope he hopes that *we* come back…I…

EMMA:

Didn't mean what you said about his extensive, arrogant ego compensating for his small—

SARAH:

NO. No, I didn't mean that.

EMMA:

You meant that you love him as much now as 18 years ago. That you need him.

SARAH:

I do.

EMMA:

I do to. Let's go home.

SARAH:

Let's make him remember. Let's make him remember why we're a family!

EMMA:

Yes…

SARAH:

How beautiful we are.

EMMA:

Yes!

SARAH:

How faultless we are as a whole even if one of us is slightly blemished. We're going back and we'll tell our Mr. that he is perfect and love is perfect and he needs us…

(We hear the phone hang up and whine a disconnected tone.)

(Sarah and Emma stop. Emma tries to cover it up, but can't turn it off. Sarah realizes Mark was on the phone the whole time. Takes the phone and listens to the dial tone.)

SARAH:

(Slowly)
Emma…you didn't. Was that…? Jesus.
(Gets up purposefully and starts the car.)

BEA:

(Entering)
Good morning, ladies. Who are we writing today?

EMMA:

The President.

BEA:

Excellent.
What?

EMMA:

(to Sarah)
What are you going to do now?

SARAH:

I'm going to Disney World.

(Emma sinks in her chair. Car peels off. Lights dim.)

- SCENE SIX -

(Five minutes later. Lights rise but only long enough to present the picture of the three women almost like a photograph. Emma hasn't moved—still sitting mouth open in bruised defeat. Sarah drives intensely, looking ahead and flustered, suddenly flips on the radio not caring what is playing. Bea is standing still, opens her mouth as if to question the situation, but decides not to. Lights fade down.)

- SCENE SEVEN -

(Twenty minutes later. Lights blink on this picture: Emma is still sitting in the same place, breathing slowly. Sarah still drives with radio on, looks back at Emma and turns around quickly, and switches radio station. Bea stands up slowly and drops Emma's diary in the passenger seat beside Sarah, walks to the back of the car lies on her bed. Lights fade.)

- SCENE NINE -

(One hour later. Lights up again on Emma sitting in the same place but balled up, head in her hands. Bea is asleep in her bed. Sarah still drives, curling the can of corn as a hand-weight)

SARAH:

ALRIGHT, Dammit.

(Stops the car. Bea wakes up.)

I'm tried of this. I'm not going to do this anymore.
Now. We are at the Florida state-line. I'm going to start driving south. If we go, we go to the ocean. But if you say so, we turn back to Maryland. I'll take you to the door and leave. You can have your father, you can have Seattle…whatever.… Whatever you need. I'll come back if you want, sometime.
So…I'll drive and if you stop me, we'll stop, turn around, and…okay.

(Silence. Bea goes to Sarah)

EMMA:

What?

SARAH:
You have to choose. You know my course.
We've still got time to get you home, to get you to Mark in time to…whatever. You need to decide for yourself if you're happy…

EMMA:
Are *you*?

SARAH:
Don't change the subject.

EMMA:
It's the same subject.

SARAH:
Just…decide.

EMMA:
Shut up. Shut up.

SARAH:
I'm trying to help. It's up to you, Bug…

EMMA:
To choose? You make me choose between two hateful people?

SARAH:
Emma. I'm trying to fix this. I want what you want but…now is the time for you to decide…I said I'll turn around whenever you say so, you have all of Florida to decide and once we get to the ocean…I don't know, we'll see what we've learned and move on, go on…

EMMA:
Keep going?

SARAH:

I don't know.

EMMA:

No. I'm not the one that has to do anything. I'm the kid, I'm both of you, I want us back, goddamn it!

SARAH:

I'm sorry.

EMMA:

Yes you are pitiful. Fuck you!

SARAH:

Emma.

EMMA:

Fuck you!

SARAH:

You are not the center of the world, Emm…

EMMA:

FUCK. YOU!

SARAH:

Fuck you too!

(Bea slaps Sarah across the face.)

BEA:

The last time my children were together was at my husband's funeral. You walked away. You walked away from your brother and I wanted to slap you then. Don't you dare walk away from her because you're scared or sorry. Or all you'll have of family is a pile of ashes. Don't wait for someone else to die before you fig-

ure that out. Nobody lives long enough to do everything, or fix everything. But there is plenty of time to do right by your family. Both of you better get this out of your system now cause if you loose each other for good...
And you are a beautiful thing and we love you like nothing else. But you are an adolescent and hard as hell to understand. You seem to know where you're going, what you want but you're off to a very lonely start. Baby, the *with* is so much more important than the *where*, trust me.
You are amazing women, but I'll tell you straight out, you need to grow up a little and you need to slow down, you both got a lot to learn and a lot of it from each other.

(Touches where she slapped Sarah's cheek. Starts to leaving for her cot)
And you should stop cussing if you're gonna be president.

(Sarah starts driving.)

EMMA:
(to no-one)
Ten miles down.

SARAH:
(to herself)
I'm not stopping.

EMMA:
50 miles...

SARAH:
I can do this...I can...

BEA:
300 miles.

SARAH:
She hasn't said anything...maybe she...

EMMA:

Slowing down.

SARAH:

Maybe she…

BEA:

We're here.

SARAH:

The coast!

BEA:

The wind.

SARAH:

The beach.

BEA:

The edge.

EMMA:

We're here.

BEA:

It's dark for 6 o-clock. The air is nervous.

SARAH:

It feels great to stop moving.

BEA:

It feels like elements are spinning.

SARAH:

We're here.

BEA:

Here knew we were coming.

SARAH:

Something's coming. A cold front.

BEA:

Cloudburst.

SARAH:

Get inside.

(Sarah and Bea move inside. Emma breaks for downstage center.)

EMMA:

(Poisonous)
Dear Mother, You are wrong. Completely and utterly, like a…wet swimsuit…you are a constranst awkward silence.
You can't sit still unless it's at 80 mph on a freeway. Running away from me and with me at the same time. Moving at the speed of light so I don't get any; At the speed of change so I can't.…I don't have real roots…I don't have real ground…I live in sand. The kind that makes this grainy and unsure, always in need of reconstruction.

SARAH:

Emma?

EMMA:

I wonder if you can help being cruel and stupid…I wonder if you can hear me…

SARAH:

I can.

EMMA:

I wonder if you can hear me saying how futile my life is now, with you…how roots belong in stillness, how I can't sleep without a motor now, how I hate this place…all places we are together. You make me wrong, you make me choose…I wonder if you know that….

SARAH:

Emma…

EMMA:

I wonder when you'll apologize to me. I wonder if you realize that I won't accept your apology if you do. I'll just run away with another piece of your broken life, another thing to chase down…

SARAH:

Emma…

EMMA:

I wonder why I want to hurt you. Do you know how much hurt that would be?

SARAH:

Emma.

EMMA:

Does Ben know?…after what you did to him, after what you're doing to me…

SARAH:

Jesus, kid.

EMMA:

And now we're here. Away from it all, with nothing in front of us but water *and it's churning*. Isn't this where you wanted? The everglades, the end of everything? And a storm is coming…your life in a hurricane.

SARAH:

Emma...

EMMA:

You drove us here hoping something would just lift you out of here. An upheaval for the soul.

SARAH:

No...

EMMA:

I could die tomorrow, you know. I could die tonight.

SARAH:

I know....

EMMA:

Does that scare you?

SARAH:

I can hear you. I can hear everything.

EMMA:

HERE is your daughter. HERE is your poet.
    (Reciting)
I've got eyes, your color, Dad's depth.
You can't see me in them, you want to forget.

You're lost without me, you've nothing but this
A road and a poem, from a life that you missed.

Ben's dead, and Bea's dying
And on you drive, on.
I'm tired of trying
Writing letters, not wrongs.

Sincerely, Emma.
> *(Emma exits.)*

SARAH:
(Runs after her)
Emma! Emma...holy shit. Emma.
> *(Picks up her diary, talking to it)*
Help me! Explain this to me, please?
> *(Looks at the urn)*
And you...What can I do for you, sir? Any answers?...Nothing.

(Alex enters on his usual rounds. Stops and waits behind Sarah.)

ALEX:
Excuse me, ma'am. Is Emma sleeping here tonight?

SARAH:
What?! Oh God. Oh my God. What...what are you...doing? Who are you?

ALEX:
I'm sorry, Ma'am. I'm Alex. I'm the one in the book.

SARAH:
This book? Her journal? You are?

ALEX:
Uh...Yes. I was worried about the weather. Maybe y'all should come inside. Is Emma sleeping already?

SARAH:
I guess...yeah. She's sleeping out here tonight. I don't know why...
Her Dad is moving to Seattle with a blonde guitar player, my homosexual brother just died and I missed the funeral, Emma tricked me into exposing my feelings of inadequacy to my husband, I refuse to return home because of it, she refuses to talk to me because of that, my mother's heart could go any second, and it looks like I've parked in a natural disaster.

ALEX:

Oh.
> *(Pause)*

Well it was nice startling you, then. I'll just…

SARAH:

No. No stay. I'm sorry for being rude. I'm the mom. I'm Sarah.

ALEX:

I know.

SARAH:

Well…this is a conversation I'm not really prepared for so…maybe we can start with casual observation about appearance: you know look very familiar. It's uncanny…really. You look exactly like…nevermind.

ALEX:

Like who? I always seem to look like someone.

SARAH:

Yeah, you have a very recognizable face.

ALEX:

Who am I?

SARAH:

Ben. My brother. He's dead.

ALEX:

I know.

SARAH:
God, that's scary. You look…like Ben. Like Ben the day he got accepted to Wake. The letter came and he told me to read it to him…you were so excited I remember, you looked just like that.
I pretended like you were rejected. I said, "oh Ben, I'm so sorry." Just to watch your face…"Just kidding babe, you're in! You made it!" And you yelled, and I yelled, and it was so funny. And you thanked me for reading it to you. Just for reading…you thanked so much, more than I ever deserved, ever. You made so much sense, your life, your friends, your school, your work, everything made the simplest kind of sense: you were happy! And I couldn't understand…why you would ruin your life with this thing…why you would do that to yourself?

ALEX:
Because I….

SARAH:
Because you what? You did it just to say to me…"I can do anything! I can be happy even when people hate me! When people misunderstand! I can do it!" Just to say to me…"give me a chance to be different and I'll do it and win. I'll win."

ALEX:
I won, didn't I?

SARAH:
Without *me*…
Remember we promised each other to live together, move to New York and rent a loft and you'd paint pictures for the Art museums, and I'd write poems about tough city life…and your wife and I would be best friends and my husband and you would take us to see shows on Broadway…remember!

ALEX:
Yes.

SARAH:

Me too. That's the only thing I do well anymore...remember things that never happened. You left me with all the things that would never happen. I should forget a few things...clean out my head, huh?

ALEX:

No.

SARAH:

I'm sorry, Ben. I'm so sorry I didn't understand, or didn't try, or didn't believe you or in you. Oh God. I'm so sorry. I lost so bad.

ALEX:

No no no...

SARAH:

Yes, I lost *you, and Emma*...and you won everything!

ALEX:

Sarah. It was my fault too. I left, I changed too.

SARAH:

I just gotta forget all that now.

ALEX:

No, Sarah.

SARAH:

Forget all that piss and blood. Fly on. Start anew. Nothing worse than lying to yourself.

ALEX:

Only when you know better.

SARAH:

I'm sorry.

ALEX:

No. No No No. You can't be. There is no room for sorry's anymore, Sarah. So your husband messed up, so your daughter vents to pillows, so you haven't figured everything out yet...I can't do that for you, but I'll be damned—and that may actual be a threat for me—but I'll risk it...cause I'll be damned if you waste your time being sorry. Sorry is for people who regret and regret is of people who've stopped...and nothing of yours is over. The brevity of my time can't distil yours.

SARAH:

I'm not worthy of it your time or mine. I lost so much already...

ALEX:

Then your penance is to never forget. That's how things die. I missed you.

SARAH:

I missed you too.
Oh Ben I'm so—

ALEX:

You're not sorry. You are not sorry. You're happy for me. Cause I'm happy for me. And I'm ecstatic for you.
    (Kisses her head)

SARAH:

What is this?

ALEX:

The air is ecstatic.

    (Emma re-enters and watched the scene like someone being betrayed.)

SARAH:
Oh God. Oh god oh god oh god. Ben! What am I gonna do with your ashes?

ALEX:
Ah…just chuck em when you get to the end.

SARAH:
The end?

ALEX:
Not too much good to me anyway, ashes. Nice pot though.

SARAH:
The end…Okay.

ALEX:
Hunker down tonight, the wind is lifting things again.

SARAH:
Ben. Can I see your journal. Your words. I want them. I want to…

ALEX:
Of course. But…don't let Emma see the graduate school part, a little R-rated. Goodnight.

SARAH:
Get Emma…check on her…

ALEX:
Sweet dreams, my lady.

(Sarah rests but does not sleep, comfortably curled like a child, thinking. Emma stands and waits as Alex passes her.)

EMMA:
Alex…Whatever she told you was wrong. She's always wrong. Alex…?

(Alex walks on. Trying something else)

Uncle Ben?

(One last try)

Dad?

ALEX:
(Finally)
Oh, I'm sorry, Emma. God it's terrible out here. Get inside. You're up?

EMMA:
I am.

ALEX:
You're crying.

EMMA:
You're here. You came. We can leave together. We can go now.

ALEX:
Oh, I'm sorry, kid. You must've misunderstood. I can't.

EMMA:
But, you're here…

ALEX:
But, you're dreaming.

EMMA:
But, you came.

ALEX:

I can't, kid. I'm sorry.

EMMA:

Don't call me that. You can't call me that…Mark.

ALEX:

Can't call me "Dad" anymore? Have I lost my title?

EMMA:

I lost, Dad. Not you.
Please take me with you. Let's go now, before it gets any worse.

ALEX:

I'm sorry, Emma.

EMMA:

But…

ALEX:

You're just dreaming?

EMMA:

Two parents, one house…that wasn't just a dream. That was real and it was perfect. Remember? Remember?

ALEX:

Wake up, Emma. There's thunder…

SARAH:

(Running out to the landing. Alex turns to Sarah)

Ben!

EMMA:

Please don't forget.

SARAH:

Ben! I've got it! I know where I'm going! I know!

ALEX:

(As Ben)
Wonderful! Lemme guess. Ah…Cote D'Azure? Casablanca? Mount Everest!

SARAH:

Back to school!

EMMA:

Please, Dad…I'm scared. The surges…

ALEX:

To school?

SARAH:

To *teach* school! I want to teach kids poetry!

ALEX:

That's perfect.

SARAH:

Isn't it! I'm going to teach them to celebrate themselves and *sing* themselves!

ALEX:

Your own herd of Whitmans!

EMMA:

I'm alone out here. I'm going back with you. You can't forget me.

(Thunder cracks, Emma jumps.)

ALEX:
(to Emma, as Dad)
That won't work, I'm sorry. I just came with your mail and a storm looks like.

EMMA:
You brought my letter.
(Grabs it and reads)

ALEX:
I know it's important to you.

EMMA:
You're important to me.

SARAH:
Ben, I can teach them everything that's important to us. Frost, Dickens, Thoreau, Angelou…math and geography if I have to. Thank you, Ben!

ALEX:
What did I do?

SARAH:
Besides making perfect sense it the midst of a tropical depression, I don't know. But I'm doing this for you. This is what I want, this is where I'm ending up!

ALEX:
A perfect end.

SARAH:
The end.

BEA:

Henry!

EMMA:

Dad!

ALEX:

(As Henry)
Yes, Dear!

BEA:

Henry, I'm tired.

ALEX:

(to Bea, as Henry)
Well, Sweet dreams, darling!

BEA:

…Of waiting. I'm tired of waiting.

EMMA:

When did it come?

ALEX:

Two days ago, I'm sorry I've got to run, kiddo.

BEA:

Henry!

SARAH:

Ben!

EMMA:

Dad! They want me to write back. They want me!

ALEX:

Who?

EMMA:

My movie stars!
    (reading)

ALEX:

    (as Dad)
Movie stars?

SARAH:

Think of it. I'm going to make throngs of little people ablaze and unforgettable!

ALEX:

    (as Ben)
I can't wait.

BEA:

I can't wait, Henry. Let's go to New York right now, just to see a show!

ALEX:

    (as Henry)
Well it's raining but…How 'bout a dance instead?

BEA:

A dance!

SARAH:

A teacher!

EMMA:

A friend! And she sent me two tickets to her movie. "I don't know when your birthday is so here is a down payment on friendship."

BEA:

(to Alex)
Should I tell Sarah and Emma before we go?

ALEX:

(as Henry)
Don't worry about it, my dear. They'll understand.

SARAH:

I've got so much to do. I can't describe it. I'm in love again…

EMMA:

"I can't describe it, I haven't written anyone since I was ten."

ALEX:

(as Ben)
It's makes the simplest kind of sense.

EMMA:

The tickets are for the movie's opening in…New York?

SARAH:

New York sounds great!

BEA:

Henry, are you ready?

ALEX:

(as Alex)
Go, Emma.
 (as Henry, offering his hand grandly)

It's getting gusty, my dear.

BEA:

My pleasure.

EMMA:

But there're only *two* tickets.

SARAH:

New people, new lives, New York.

ALEX:

(as Ben)
Never forget, Sarah.

EMMA:

(Getting upset)
But there are only two tickets.

SARAH:

(Remembering)
Emma.

EMMA:

Mom, there are only two...two...
(Looking for Bea)

SARAH:

Emma.

EMMA:

Bea?

(Sarah joins Emma, both looking at Bea.)

SARAH:

Momma?

(No answer as music starts, thunder rolls, Alex and Bea dance)

EMMA:

Grandma?...You still breathing?

BEA:

(Laughs joyfully, more thunder.)

(Alex and Bea dance and spin. As Emma and Sarah watch blissfully, Sarah weakens and relaxes to her knees, crying.)

(Music fades, lights down on the dancers. A spot is still shining on Emma and Sarah. They look at each other.)

EMMA:

I don't...want to be a kid anymore.

SARAH:

Okay. I don't much want to be a grownup...I guess that leaves us as either friends or enemies.

EMMA:

Or strangers.

SARAH:

And I guess that depends on where were are.

EMMA:

Or where we're going.

(Silence. Emma reaches for Sarah's hand. Lights shift to downstage, there is no blackout.)

- Epilogue -

(Emma walks into the light, Sarah watches from another spot. Relaxed, informal.)

EMMA:

P.S.

And the storm blew us, but never away. For there is a strength found only in the siege. Passed down by generations of women-tempests that make tough acts to follow.

We did go to New York, Mom and I, just to see a show. Traveling first through storms and the parts of the South they call deep to emphasize its forgiving qualities, its penchant for reconstruction. We also made our way through parts of the heart they call deep to emphasize the same.

For there is an urgency in living that allows for imperfection, impossibility, celebrity, poetry, Airmail, and Winnebagoes. I recommend all of the above.

Sincerely, Emma Macy

(Lights down slowly to black.)

- THE END -

978-0-595-37966-8
0-595-37966-4

Made in the USA
Lexington, KY
20 October 2017